Harlow's Humor

THE DEVIL'S HANDMAIDENS MC: ATLANTIC CITY, NJ CHAPTER

ANDI RHODES

BLUE JOURNEY PUBLISHING

Also by Andi Rhodes

Broken Rebel Brotherhood

Broken Souls

Broken Innocence

Broken Boundaries

Broken Rebel Brotherhood: Complete Series Box set

Broken Rebel Brotherhood: Next Generation

Broken Hearts

Broken Wings

Broken Mind

Bastards and Badges

Stark Revenge

Slade's Fall

Jett's Guard

Soulless Kings MC

Fender

Joker

Piston

Greaser

Riker

Trainwreck

Squirrel

Gibson

Satan's Legacy MC

Snow's Angel

Toga's Demons

Magic's Torment

Prologue

HARLOW

Ten years ago…

"WE HAVE another winner here at the Devil's Double Down…"

I roll my eyes and ignore the rest of the announcement. I've heard it hundreds and hundreds of times in my life. When I was younger, I loved it. Loved the pinging of the machines, the way old ladies came in and lost their shit when they won any amount of money. It was fascinating to me.

But now I'm sixteen and there are more important things in life than bright lights and clanging machines. Like why my mom has me stuffed in this stupid room instead of watching her handle business. She's always told me that I'll take over one day: the casino, the club, the family. So it makes no sense to me why I'm stuck behind the glass of her upstairs office, watching everything from a distance.

"Club business" was the only answer she gave me when I asked her for an explanation. Oh yeah, did I mention my mom is the president of the Atlantic City, New Jersey chapter of an all female motorcycle club? The Devil's Handmaidens MC to be exact. The baddest bitches in the state, in the country really, and I'm one of them. Or I will be someday, when I'm 'old enough' and 'ready'.

I flip my hatchet end over end as I stare at the blue-hairs below, my eyes tracking everything going on in the casino. I'm never without my hatchet. Unless I'm at school. Those pricks don't let us bring in anything fun.

Anyway, I'm babysitting. I'm fucking babysitting the casino. Mom tells me it's an important job, just as important, if not more, than anything else the club does. But all it is to me is a noose around my neck holding me back from doing what I really want to do. Be a part of real club business.

My lips tip up into a grin, but it quickly slips when I try to picture exactly what real club business looks like. Because the truth of the matter is, I don't know. I've grown up in the club, around the members and officers. I've been exposed to more than most young girls. And I've also been shielded, protected.

Lillith Monroe, aka Velvet, wanted her daughter to have a normal life, or as normal as possible under the club's wing. I was read bedtime stories, taken to the park, had tea parties, and played dress up. Granted, my tea parties and dress up consisted of leather and pretend liquor, but I was still allowed to be a little girl.

As I got older, my toys changed from dollhouses and tea sets to poker chips and hatchets. I no longer wanted to ride my Barbie bicycle because I wanted my two wheels to look like everyone else's: black and chrome with the Harley emblem proudly displayed. I didn't want to walk around the casino floor anymore and have my cheeks pinched by our customers. No, I wanted to be the one doing the pinching.

I glance at the steel blade with its custom wrapped leather handle in my hands, and my grin returns. Rising up from the worn-out chair that faces the glass overlook, I whirl around and launch my weapon at the target next to the door.

As it sails through the air, the door swings open, and I squeal. The Sergeant at Arms of DHMC, Tahiti, cuts her gaze to the hatchet that missed her by inches.

"Fucking hell, Velvet needs to move this goddamn target before one of her own ends up dead," Tahiti says before turning to look at me, her hand still on the doorknob. "What's got you in a funk?"

I flop down into the chair and cross my arms over my chest, huffing out a breath in the process. "Babysitting."

Tahiti smiles a knowing smile. Bitch hates this post as much as I do. The difference is, she's not usually stuck with it because she's needed for club business.

"Two years, Har," she says, like she always does. "You've got two fucking years until you can prospect. Let's try to stay out of juvie until then, yeah?"

She reaches with her free arm and yanks the hatchet out of the wall. Her eyes rake over the sweet-sixteen gift my mom bought me two months ago. All the members were envious of the custom piece when I lifted it out of the box at my birthday party, and so far, Tahiti is the only one who hasn't gone out and purchased one for herself.

"Yeah, yeah," I grumble.

Tahiti stares at me for a moment before she grins. "Wanna get out of here?"

Immediately, I sit up a little straighter. "Do motorcycles have handlebars?"

Her spiky blonde hair doesn't move an inch as she throws her head back and laughs.

When she sobers, there's a fire in her eyes that wasn't there a second ago. "Seriously though, Velvet wanted me to come get you."

My excitement diminishes. "What's she need me to do now? Go take out the trash or something?"

"Or something." Tahiti thrusts the hatchet in my direction. "C'mon, Har. You're gonna need this."

I leap from the chair and cross the room as fast as I can, taking my blade from her. If I'm gonna need this, it can't be something too bad, right?

I follow Tahiti down the hallway toward the back staircase, the one that leads to the basement of the casino. My heartbeat quickens the closer we get because I've never been allowed into the basement.

Calm down, Harlow. You might not be going all the way down.

"So, how's school going?" Tahiti asks as she pushes open the stairwell door.

"Eh."

She glances at me over her shoulder. "Oh, c'mon, Har. It can't be that bad."

I shrug. "It's school, T. Nothing special."

"Isn't the Spring dance coming up?"

I groan. "Next weekend."

"Got a date yet?"

"Hell no. I'm not going."

"Seriously?" She stops with her foot hovering above the next step and turns to face me. "Why?"

I lift my hatchet and smirk. "Not exactly a ton of guys lining up to ask me."

Tahiti shakes her head and grins. "They don't know what they're missing." Her eyes lower until she takes in my still growing cleavage, and then lower still to the shorts I'm wearing. "Not that you're trying to hide any of it."

"It's just a stupid dance, T. I don't wanna go anyway. I'd rather be at the clubhouse."

That's true, to a point. I love being at the clubhouse. And it *is* a stupid dance. But shit, I wanna go. Not alone, though.

"Whatever you say."

Tahiti doesn't push and continues down the steps. I try to suppress my shock when we pass the door for the first level, but it's impossible. The burst of air rushes past my lips, despite my pressing them together.

"Don't get too excited," Tahiti says over her shoulder. "Once you see what's down here, you can never unsee it."

There's something in her tone that causes my stomach to clench. Tahiti takes her job as SAA seriously, but nothing ever seems to phase her. But whatever we're walking toward, whatever is behind that all elusive door I've never been able to breach… it unnerves her, pulls her to a dark side she rarely displays around me.

When we reach the door, I stand next to Tahiti in the narrow hallway. She pulls her badge out from between her tits and holds it up to the lock pad. A soft beep fills the space around us, and the lock disengages as she tucks the card back into the safety of her double-Ds.

With both her hands on the door to push it open, Tahiti pauses and glances at me. "Brace yourself, Har."

And I do. Because the mixture of equal parts excitement and trepidation have me practically vibrating out of my skin. And if I'm being let in on whatever the hell this is, I have no time for giving in to either.

Tahiti pushes the door all the way open, and I'm greeted by a sight that will forever change my life. I don't know how, but I know it will. The sight will be emblazoned on my brain, in my soul, until I take my dying breath.

Because staring back at me, through the stink of desperation and suffering, are the eyes of dozens of girls—few appear older than me, but I'd bet my Harley savings that most are my age or younger—who look scared for their lives.

"What the fuck is going on?" I snap, stomping to my mom, who I spot next to a cot a few feet away.

"Club business, Har," she replies calmly, quietly.

I watch my mother's actions as she covers up a girl who can't be more than ten or eleven with a blanket. She brushes the girl's hair out of her face, like she used to do to me, and whispers, "You're safe now, sweetie. Close your eyes and try to rest."

Mom grabs me by the elbow and practically drags me to the side of the room. I look around until my eyes land on Tahiti, now standing by the exit, a jittery glint in her eyes.

"Harlow," Mom says, pulling my attention back to her. "I need you to stay here, with some of the members, and help with these girls."

"Where'd they come from, Mom? What's going on?"

Mom tips her head back and blows out a breath. When she brings her gaze back to me, her eyes soften. "I wanted to keep you away from this until you were eighteen, when you'd be at least old enough to prospect." She pauses, but I don't speak. Her eyes leave mine for a minute, maybe two, as she looks out over the rows of cots, all full. When she looks at me again, her eyes are hard. She's Velvet now, not Mom or Lillith. All Velvet. "These girls were being trafficked for sex."

I gasp. It's not like I didn't know the world was fucked up, or that things like this happened, but I never for a moment dreamed it was happening under our noses or at our doorstep. All that protection I had, I suppose.

"Okay."

"Tahiti and I, and a few others, need to go back out."

"But why?" I suddenly don't want her to leave. I want her to stay, with me, where she's safe.

Mom grips my shoulders. "Harlow, listen to me," she snaps. "I have to do what I have to do. And that means you need to step up now and help take care of these girls. I need you. *They* need you."

I swallow past the lump in my throat and nod. "Okay, Mom."

"Good."

She presses a kiss to my forehead, lingering a little too long, and my eyes close of their own accord. She hasn't done that in forever. This must be bad. She turns to walk away from me, but I grab her wrist to stop her.

"Can you at least tell me where you're going?" I ask, fearing I'll get the same stock answer I always do.

A grin appears on her face, one that promises pain and suffering for those who cross her. Velvet, president of the DHMC: Atlantic City, NJ chapter is on full display in that grin.

"To take out the fuckers we rescued them from," she says coldly, swinging her arm to indicate the room.

With that, she walks toward Tahiti, toward the path to justice. I watch her go, but when the sun bursts through the opening exit door, I call out to her.

"I love—"

The door slams shut in her and Tahiti's wake.

You.

CHAPTER 1

Harlow

PRESENT DAY...

"WE CAN'T SAVE them all, Har."

I stare through the glass at the casino floor below, not bothering to look at Tahiti. She's no longer our SAA because she wanted to step down once new blood arrived at the club, but she will always be the woman who was my mom's best friend and the closest thing I have to family now.

A long sigh fills the office, the one that's now mine. As the president of the Devil's Handmaidens MC: Atlantic City, NJ chapter, I've earned it. But sometimes I hate it as much as I did back at sixteen. There are too many memories tied to it, too much emotion. And not all of it good.

"Har, talk to me," Tahiti presses when I remain silent.

"She'd have saved them," I spit out.

I watch her reflection in the glass as Tahiti walks toward me, and my knuckles protest when I squeeze the hatchet in my hand. I don't want her wisdom right now. The pain is too raw, too new, too exposed.

As if she senses my need for space, Tahiti halts, bringing her arms to cross over her chest.

"You're just like her, ya know?" she says quietly.

My shoulders tense, along with the rest of my body. I

know I look like my mom, the late, great Velvet. I see her every time I look in a goddamn mirror. But I'm not her. My chest tightens like it always does at the thought of the woman who gave me life.

"Not alike enough, though, right?" I counter sardonically. Slowly turning, I twist the hatchet blade in my hand. "Don't quite fill those particular shoes, do I?"

Before I can give Tahiti a piece of my mind for the pity in her eyes, the door bursts open, and Peppermint, my VP, rushes in. She skids to a stop as her gaze collides with mine, no doubt seeing my ire.

"Not again," she grumbles.

Tahiti darts her eyes back and forth between me and Peppermint before she takes a deep breath and exhales. She focuses on my VP and forces a smile.

"I guess I'm being tagged out."

"I can come—"

"It's fine, Peppermint," Tahiti pushes out. "You're her best friend. Maybe you can talk some sense into her."

"I'm right fucking here," I snap, annoyed at them acting as if I'm invisible.

Tahiti walks out of the room, shaking her head, without saying anything else. Good, one less concerned look for me to deal with. When we're alone, Peppermint walks across the room and leans against the glass wall.

"So, wanna talk about it?" she asks.

"Nope."

I move to my desk and sit in the cushy leather chair I splurged on a few months ago. It was a treat to myself after being dumped by Jack. Fucker wanted something I couldn't give, something I'll never be able to give.

After setting my hatchet down, I shift through some of the paperwork, searching for the week's invoices and trying to focus my mind on something else, anything else. Peppermint pushes off the wall and strides to sit in one of the chairs opposite me. I glance up and see her not-gonna-let-this-go expression and heave a sigh.

"Spit it out, Pep. I know you want to say something."

She leans forward and rests her elbows on the desk. Her mouth opens and closes several times, telling me she's trying to find the words. She's not always like this, so indecisive. Hell, she can't be, not when she's the VP. But when it comes to conversations between just the two of us, she tends to overthink, get in her head and bring emotion into things.

It's been that way since the day I met her. That day ten years ago when I watched my mother cover her with a blanket and tell her that she was safe. And when my mother didn't come home like she said she would, I promised myself that I'd make sure I kept her word.

"How many rescue missions have we gone on together?" she asks.

I shrug. "You'd have to ask Story," I tell her, referring to our club secretary.

"One twenty-seven."

My head snaps up. "What?"

"We've gone on one hundred and twenty-seven rescue missions together."

"If you knew the answer, why'd you ask?"

"Because I need *you* to know the answer. Because I need *you* to remember that number, to remember the faces of every single person you've saved."

I wave a hand dismissively, wanting no part of this conversation. "You looked like you were on a mission when you came in here. Did you need something?"

Peppermint huffs out a laugh, but it's without humor. "Harlow Monroe, master of avoidance." She reaches across the desk and grabs my hand. "You saved me, Har. If ever you need a reminder of all the good you're doing, look at me."

"Velvet saved you," I push out.

"Velvet rescued me, but you saved me. There's a difference."

I pull my hand away. "What did you need, Pep? I've got a fucking shitload of paperwork to get to."

"Just let me say one more thing and then I'll drop it."

She stares at me, waiting for permission. I give her a single nod and can see the relief in her eyes, which only serves to make my chest tighten more. If ever there's a person in this world that I don't want to disappoint or hurt, it's this bitch.

"I love you, Har. Always will."

Those words take the wind out of my sails. "Fucking hell, Pep. You know I can't—"

Peppermint holds a hand up. "I know you can't say it back. And that's okay. I know how you feel. I just needed to remind you that you aren't alone. That even though we can't save them all, we still save hundreds. And that's because of you."

I want to argue, to tell her that today's failure blurs the faces of those we've saved, but I can't. Because how do you say that kinda thing to a person in her position? She's living proof that DHMC does great things. She's a daily reminder of why I fight so hard to fill my mother's impossibly giant shoes, why every chapter of DHMC does what they do, by whatever means necessary.

"Thanks, bitch," I settle on.

Her face lights up with a smile, and my nerves settle. Yeah, she's the reason, my reason.

"Now, back to what you needed," I urge.

"Right, well…"

The smile is gone, in its place a steely determination. When she's not trying to pull me out of a funk or forcing me to face feelings I don't want to face, Peppermint is one tough cookie and the only person I'd want at my side running this club. She's fierce, loyal, and the slightest bit twisted.

Slightest? She's fucking nuts.

"Mr. Ricci is here."

So much for my nerves settling. My hand immediately goes to my hatchet, needing the weight of it in my grasp to center me.

"What does he want?"

Peppermint shrugs. "Says he wants to talk business."

"Business my ass. He knows he can't be here."

"Well, he refused to leave, said he'd only talk to you. I put him in the conference room." She grins. "Locked him in, actually."

I turn to my tablet and tap the screen to wake it up. After typing in my password, I tap on the security icon and the conference room fills the screen. I narrow my eyes at the Armani wearing cunt sitting at the head of the long mahogany table.

"Looks like he's made himself comfortable," I mumble, turning the screen so Peppermint can see.

"I think it's about time you show him who owns that particular seat," she says, humorous evil in her tone.

"I think you're right."

I push up from my chair, secure my hatchet in the sheath on my hip, and then cross the room to the door. Just before my hand grips the knob, Peppermint's voice stops me.

"Uh, Prez, ya gonna clean the blood off your face, maybe change?"

Glancing down at myself, I take in the crimson stains on my jeans and the blood splatter on my white t-shirt. My leather cut completes the look, with its green and black patches, the patches that let everyone know who I am.

I look at her over my shoulder and smirk. "Nope."

Her evil grin widens. "I was hoping you'd say that." She rubs her hands together in front of her like a pedophile at the park.

I stride out the door and down the hallway toward the main stairwell, Peppermint on my heels. I could use the elevator, but why bother? I'd rather keep Mr. Ricci waiting, even if it's only for a minute or two longer.

Fucking Malachi Ricci. Owner of Umbria's Universe and heir to the throne of the Ricci Crime Family. And apparently the prick who thinks he can sit at the head of *my* table because the rules don't apply to him.

He's about to get a lesson in knowing his place. A lesson I'm looking forward to teaching him.

Entitled, rich bitch motherfucker.

CHAPTER 2
Malachi

I GLANCE at the clock on the wall and barely contain the growl threatening to tear from my throat. Twelve minutes. That's how long it's been since that leather-wearing ginger told me to have a seat while she went to get her boss. Or should I say, how long it's been since the bitch *locked* me in here like I'm some common street thug who can't be trusted?

Ha! She need only look in a mirror to find one of those. Bikers, street thugs… same thing, right?

Remember why you're here, Mal.

My fingertips beat out a steady drum on the table-top, in time with my bouncing leg. Making me wait like this is unacceptable, and I plan on schooling them in just how abhorrent I find it. I've no doubt people don't keep my father waiting this long.

My father, Antonio Ricci, don of the Ricci Crime Family, would be tearing this room apart by now. He doesn't suffer fools, and it's a fool for sure who doesn't respect his time. And if you think his son, a Capo under his reign, is immune to this, think again. I've had black eyes, split lips, and loose teeth… and that was just the times I was a *minute* late to something he deemed important.

Footsteps outside the door have me spinning the chair around, glancing at my Rolex as I do. Twenty-Two minutes. I was shoved in this room for a full twenty-two minutes, and I'm fuming.

I rise from my seat and button my suit jacket as I watch the door fly open only to bounce off the wall. Narrowing my eyes, I glare at the woman now occupying the space. She's a tiny brunette wearing a fuck you smirk. Her eyes are emerald pools of fury, and her petite frame reminds me of a stacked pixie. And despite the blood she's covered in, she's making it almost impossible to remember why I'm here.

Harlow Monroe, bane of my existence, is goddamn gorgeous.

And a biker. Daddy dearest would not approve, not that I give a shit about that anymore. I shake my head in an attempt to loosen the thoughts and bring my reason for being here back into the forefront.

"It's about ti—"

"What do you want?" she snaps, and my annoyance flares back to life, the hold her lethal beauty had on me gone.

I shove my hands in my pockets to keep from reaching out and strangling her. I'm here to conduct business, not murder. Although murder is slowly working its way to the top of my to-do list.

I take a deep breath, hold it for five seconds, and slowly exhale. "I've come to make a proposition."

Harlow drops her eyes in a blatant perusal of my body that would have lesser men coming in their pants. Her nostrils flare, and her fingers twitch at her sides. "Not interested."

I smirk at her, not letting her get even a whiff that her words sting. Women normally can't resist me, even if it's for no other reason than my power. But this girl, this biker bitch, doesn't seem the least bit affected by me. And for some reason that irks me, makes me want to do whatever it takes to win her over. No one has had that effect on me in way too long. Not since…

Stupid. Plain fucking stupid.

"Funny," I say. "But I was talking about actual business." I run my eyes over her body, much like she did mine, paying extra attention to the cleavage pillowing above her bloody top. "Not that I couldn't be persuaded into a side venture."

Harlow's cheeks inflame, but her hand moves to the hatchet on her hip, and she grips the handle. "You've got five seconds to tell me what you want. And seeing as you shouldn't be here in the first place, that's generous."

I arch a brow. "Sticking to business. I like it." I turn to gesture at the table and surrounding chairs. "If you'll have a seat, I'd be happy to explain my presence to you."

Turning away from Harlow, I ignore her angry huff and grip the arms of my chair to pull it toward me to sit down. Before my ass hits the leather cushion, I'm halted by a tight arm around my neck and a blade pressed into the flesh just above said arm.

"That's my seat," Harlow snarls in my ear. "And this is my turf. You'd do well to remember that, *Mr. Ricci.*"

The way she sneers my name, like it's worse than acid on her tongue, boils my blood. And the heat from her arm against me only fuels the fire. I wrap my fingers around her forearm in an attempt to guide her away from my throat, but she doesn't budge.

"It's Malachi," I say calmly. "Mr. Ricci is my father."

"I don't give a flying fuck," she hisses as she drags me toward a different chair.

When she pushes me down into it, her arm slides away, but the edge of the hatchet remains. Harlow sits on the edge of the chair I'd been using, her weapon carefully raised in front of her as she glares at me. It isn't until she scoots her chair to the table that she rests her hatchet on the wooden top.

I could reach out and take it, show her I'm not someone

she can intimidate, or handle for that matter, but I decide against it. She's right, this is her turf. I'd have done the same thing had she shown up at Umbria's Universe, especially considering the treaty in place. Doesn't mean it doesn't piss me off, though.

The woman who locked me in this room to begin with moves from the doorway, closing it behind her, and sits across from me. Funny, my attention had been so focused on Harlow that I hadn't noticed the bitch was even present.

"I believe Harlow gave you five seconds to tell us what you want," she says. "Seeing as that time is up, you should probably start talking."

"And you are?" I arch a brow.

"Absolutely right," Harlow answers for her.

I smooth my hands down my lapels. You'd think with the life I've had, a life dedicated to my father and his orders, I'd be used to demands and shitty attitudes. And I am… from men. When it comes to women who are pint-size with the personality of a bull in a china shop… not so much.

"Right, well." I clear my throat. "As you know, I own Umbria's Universe. Not only is it the most upscale casino in Atlantic City, but it also promises to be the most successful."

Harlow leans back in her chair and crosses her arms over her chest. "I don't deal in promises. I deal in facts." The corners of her lips pull up into a grin. "And the fact is, Devil's Double Down has been, and will remain, the best casino around. We might not be fancy—obnoxiously so, I might add —but I couldn't give two shits about that. We're the best and that's what matters."

I bristle at her words, annoyed that they have such an effect on me. I realize they wouldn't have an impact if they were lies, but what she says is true. For years, Devil's Double Down has cornered the market on casino business, and I need that to change. Fast.

"And that's why I'm here."

I reach into my pocket and pull out the slip of paper I wrote on before coming here. I slide it across the table toward Harlow. She stares at it for a long moment, almost as if trying to determine if it'll blow up when she touches it, but then she picks it up. Her eyes widen a fraction as she reads the figure, but otherwise, she's expressionless before she hands it to the only other person in the room.

"This is a joke, right?" the woman asks, incredulously.

Without taking her eyes off of me, Harlow responds to her friend. "Something tells me it's not, Peppermint."

Peppermint? What the fuck kinda name is that?

"It's not a joke, I assure you," I tell them. "I want to buy the Devil's Double Down, and as you can see, I'm willing to pay well above what it's worth." I nod toward the slip of paper.

Harlow throws her head back and laughs, actually fucking laughs. My shoulders tense, and my blood seems to thicken in my veins with outrage.

"I fail to see the humor."

Harlow continues laughing but Peppermint simply rolls her eyes before addressing me. "The humor, *Malachi*, is that you think we'd ever sell. Or, more accurately, that you think we'd sell to *you*."

My eyes dart back and forth between the two women as I decide how to best play my wild card. I don't want to play it, not one bit. But I'm starting to think I'm not going to have a choice.

"Miss Monroe," I begin once she's stopped laughing. "I think it would be in your best interest to, at the very least, consider my offer. Imagine the things you could do with that kind of money."

Harlow's face hardens, all evidence of her earlier hysterics gone. "You can't put a price tag on some things," she says coldly. "And the fact that you're here, trying to do just that, is fucking offensive."

I lift my hands, palms out. "No offense meant, *cara amica*. This is—"

"I am not your friend," Harlow snarls as she stands up so fast her chair rolls back and hits the wall. "And I don't appreciate you coming in here like some, some, *farfallone*, who can sweet talk his way into getting what he wants."

If it were possible for my brows to touch my hairline, I have no doubt they would right now. I didn't expect Harlow to know any Italian, much less enough to throw insults back at me.

Harlow leans on the table so her face is inches from mine. "The only reason you're not already dead on this floor is because I actually honor the treaty our parents signed. Clearly, you don't. Now get out of my casino."

I stand from my chair and curl my hands over its back before pushing it under the table. It's time for my wild card.

"Miss Monroe, take the money." My tone is calm, not giving even the slightest betrayal of the turmoil rolling through me at seeing the anguish that flashed in her eyes at the mention of the treaty. She sees me as her enemy, and I'm not. But I can't tell her that, not yet. Instead, I have to twist the knife a little more, push forward when part of me knows I should retreat. "The last thing you want is your stubborn pride to cause a war. And that's exactly what you'll get if you refuse." I move to the door and pull it open. "You have forty-eight hours to make a decision. I'll be in touch."

With that, I disappear down the hallway, leaving Harlow Monroe to think about her decision. And every step I take brings more nerves, more fear that she'll make the wrong choice.

Because that will have fatal consequences for us both.

CHAPTER 3

Harlow

"EVERYONE'S HERE, HAR."

I spare Peppermint a glance as I stride toward the worn-out target on my office wall. Gripping my hatchet, I yank it out of the bullseye. As soon as Malachi Ricci left, I called church. I don't keep anything from my sisters, least of all an attempt to take what's ours or a threat against us.

And then I'd promptly come here to obliterate the images the man caused to taunt my mind… and my libido. Pretentious asshole is a sexy bundle of sin and aggravation. What's worse is, as much as I hate him, I'm filled with equal parts of wanting him. The way he talks, his self-assurance, the way his eyes darkened when he glided them over my body… it pissed me the fuck off and sparked a fire between my legs at the same time.

I shake off the thoughts and fully face my VP, praying the heat spreading through my veins isn't apparent on my face.

"Who's gonna watch the casino floor?" I ask.

My best friend eyes me skeptically, but wisely doesn't comment on what, if anything, she sees. "A few of the girls are, the ones who've gone through the full training curriculum."

I nod. The 'girls' she's referring to are some of the ones we've rescued from a life of being trafficked. Every rescue mission ends the same. We give each individual the choice of what they want to do next. Most want to go home, and we make sure that happens because we don't want anyone here that doesn't want to be here. Fuck, their choices were taken away once, and I refuse to do it again.

But there are a few who decide to stay because they have no home to return to. And if they stay, they earn their keep. Whether by working at the casino, working as an escort, or opting to prospect for the club. All those who stay go through the training to cover the casino floor because we never know when we'll need them for it.

"Tahiti is staying in the basement with the latest arrivals."

I lock my eyes on Peppermint. "She's not coming to church?"

Tahiti isn't required to be at church, not since she's retired from being our SAA, but she rarely misses.

Peppermint shrugs. "Said she figures Spooks being present is enough."

Spooks, our new SAA, is a transfer from our Portland, Oregon chapter. When Luna, that chapter's president, called me and explained the shit Spooks went through, there was zero hesitation when I extended the invite to our chapter. After approval was received from Brazen, our mother chapter president, Spooks officially became an Atlantic City sister.

I huff out a laugh. "The day Spooks isn't enough is the day I'll hang up my cut. Bitch is crazy."

"Yeah," Peppermint agrees, a wide grin on her face. "In the best possible ways."

Shaking my head, I sheath my hatchet and lead us both out the door and down the hallway to the elevator that will take us back to the conference room. We have two locations where we hold church. The conference room, here at the casino, is used when we need to meet quickly during the day and most of us are here anyway. And then there's the club-house, which is located on the outskirts of the city.

I'd much prefer the clubhouse, but some things just can't wait.

When I open the door to the conference room, an image of Malachi standing at the table flashes through my mind. I freeze as unwelcome tingles dance along my spine.

This is not the time for fantasies that can never be acted upon.

The chatter of my officers dies down, and silence fills the room. The table is surrounded by a sea of women wearing leather cuts adorned with green and black patches and *fuck-you-very-much* expressions. Perfect.

"Lay it on us, Prez," Mama says.

I whip my head in my enforcer's direction, narrowing my eyes slightly. "Have a seat and I'll get started." Everyone sits, but I remain standing. I shift my gaze to each of my sisters, telling them with my eyes how important this is. "First, thank you all for coming. I know this is last minute, but that should give you some indication as to how imperative it is that we meet."

"Are we going on another rescue mission?" Giggles, our road captain, asks. "Might need a little time to plan, seeing as we just finished one this morning."

"No, it's not another rescue mission, although you know as well as I do that we do those when we have to, regardless of the amount of time we have to prep."

"I know, it's just…"

"What?" I snap.

Giggles looks down at her hands for a brief moment before lifting her gaze back up to meet mine. "This morning was a cluster fuck. We lost more than we should have." I watch her throat work as she swallows, sadness taking over. "It's hard, ya know? Every time we lose a little boy, I think of Noah."

Noah is Giggles' little brother. He's ten and the only

family she has left in the world, other than the club. I know she struggles more than the rest of us with each victim we can't save. And this morning was particularly brutal as most of the people we were hired to rescue were already dead when we arrived. We were too late.

I take a deep breath, holding it in while I try to come up with the words to make this okay for Giggles, okay for all of us. But there aren't any.

"Listen, all of you. I know what we do is brutal. I know that we sometimes lose more than we save. Today was one of those times." I feel like I'm lying, because I was broken when we returned from this morning's mission. But these women look to me for direction, and if that means I have to lie about how I feel, so be it. "When we struggle, when the heartbreak feels like it's too much to bear, we have to remember those we did help. And all you have to do to remind yourself of them is look around you. We're surrounded by people we've gotten out of hell."

I look at Peppermint out of the corner of my eye, needing to see my own personal reminder, my reason for doing what I do. She's smirking, no doubt thinking about our conversation earlier today. She knows I'm putting on a front, but she'd never call me out on it.

"Can we cut the feelings bullshit and get back to the reason we're here?" Spooks asks just before glancing at Giggles. "Sorry. Not trying to minimize your shit, but Prez is right. We can't change what happened this morning. So why hash it out?"

"Spooks has a point," Mama says. "Why don't we all get some time in at the targets tonight, work out some aggression from this morning?"

The targets were something I set up shortly after my mom gave me my hatchet. It's an outdoor space that we can practice ax throwing, or anything that has a blade throwing for that matter. I love the space, and when Spooks arrived, she was thrilled to see it, as they had a target set up at her old chapter.

"That sounds like a plan," I say. "It's not mandatory, but if you're struggling from this morning, feel free."

"If I can get someone to stay with Noah, I'm in," Giggles says.

"Bring him to the clubhouse. I'm sure Tahiti would love to see him."

Giggles chuckles. Tahiti acts like a grandma to Noah. A young, badass grandma. "Done."

"Good." I nod. "Now, back to business." I inhale deeply and let the air rush out past my lips. "Malachi Ricci paid me a visit after we got back this morning."

"Seriously? He knows he can't be here. What the fuck did he want?" Story asks, sitting forward in her chair to lean on the table.

I reach into my pocket for the slip of paper with Malachi's offer on it. I set it on the table and slide it toward Peppermint. Since she's already seen it, she passes it on.

While my sisters are looking at the figure, I explain. "He wants to buy Devil's Double Down." Protests and outrage erupt so I hold up my hand to silence them all. "Fucker's given me forty-eight hours to let him know my decision. Of course I already told him the casino isn't for sale, no matter what obscene amount of money he wants to throw at me." My jaw clenches as I remember Malachi's thinly veiled threat. "But him wanting to buy us out isn't the problem."

"Not even close," Peppermint mutters.

"As if that's not bad enough," Spooks spits out.

"Unfortunately, it does get worse. He made it clear he doesn't give a shit about the peace treaty just by showing up, but he also threatened a war if I don't accept his offer."

"You've gotta be kidding me," Giggles snarls.

"I wish," I tell her. "Obviously, I don't want a war, but I refuse to bend to his will. That treaty means something, to all of us, and we've followed it to the letter for the last ten years. But I'll be damned if I'm going to cower to some rich bitch simply because he says so. I need you to all be aware of what's coming. We've gone up against some pretty nasty motherfuckers, but something tells me that the Italians are different. So, keep an eye out, pay attention to law enforcement and what's on their radar, and for the love of God, don't go anywhere alone. He gave me forty-eight hours, but I don't trust it."

"I'm not worried about law enforcement," Mama spits out. "We've got enough of them on our payroll. But the Italians? Har, that didn't work out so well last time. What makes you think it'll work any better this time?"

I heave a sigh and pull my hatchet out to give my hands something to do. "I don't know… yet. But we'll do what we have to do."

"Fuck yes we will," Spooks agrees and turns to Mama. "We're stronger than we were before. We can take them."

I agree, but I'm not stupid. The Italians won't fight fair. Malachi's defiance of the treaty is proof of that. We have to be smart about this, find their weak spot. Once we do that, they won't stand a chance against us.

I focus on our secretary and tech guru. "Story, I need you to find whatever you can on Malachi and Umbria's Universe. Dig as deep as you need to and put together a report for tomorrow night. I want to know everything." I adjust my stance so I can address everyone. "We'll meet again tomorrow night, seven o'clock, at the clubhouse. Come prepared to be there for a while."

"I'll talk to Tahiti and make sure she can watch Noah," Peppermint tells Giggles. "If she can't or would prefer to be in church, I'm sure one of the other girls can."

Mama smiles at her. "Thanks."

"Dismissed," I say to the group. "If you come to the targets, I'll see ya later. If you don't, have a good night. And get some fucking sleep. I have a feeling we're gonna need all we can get before shit really hits the fan."

CHAPTER 4
Malachi

"WHAT THE FUCK WERE YOU THINKING?"

I glare at my father from across the room. He beckoned me in here ten minutes ago, demanding a report about my visit to Devil's Double Down. The great Antonio Ricci is a skeleton of his former self, his body riddled with cancer. My father is knocking on death's door, and still, he knows how to pull my strings like the puppet master he is.

I fucking hate it, hate him. But I need to keep up appearances, especially in the presence of my Uncle Angelo and cousin, Nicholi.

"Answer him," Uncle Angelo seethes.

I pinch the bridge of my nose and squeeze my eyes shut. I've had several hours to come up with an explanation for my threat to Harlow, none of which will be acceptable to these men. And the truth isn't an option. The truth hasn't been an option for the last six years.

"I was thinking that we need to stop pussyfooting around and shut them down," I say, with conviction. "I was thinking that, if we want to have complete control of the city, we need to take out the Devil's Handmaidens MC. We've let a goddamn piece of paper hold us back for too long."

"You can't be that stupid," Nicholi spits out. "We're in no position for a war." He nods at my father. "Not right now. You just opened us up to all kinds of trouble."

"And they're not stupid either," I snap, annoyed at being spoken to by my cousin like that. He might be a Capo, like me, but I'm still the don's son. And he needs to respect that fact, whether he likes it or not. "They won't opt for a war. It would expose them in ways they can't afford."

Not that I really think a silly thing like optics will stop them. I hope it doesn't stop them.

"Get out."

I whip my head back to my father. "Excuse me?"

"You heard me," he grits out. "Get. Out."

I swing my gaze to each of the three men before huffing out a breath. "You know I made the right call. You're just too blind to see it." I turn on my heel and stride out of the room.

Only when I'm in the hallway do I allow myself to lower my guard. I unbutton the cuffs of my button-down and roll my sleeves up as I stride toward the front door. I need to get out of here, get away from the overwhelming sense of failure this house brings down on me.

My shoes crunch on the white gravel my father insisted upon using for his driveway. It's ugly, especially against the ostentatious estate, but it's just another way for him to exert control. No fucker would dare come barreling in the driveway at a disrespectful speed and risk kicking up rocks and dirt to sully their expensive vehicles.

I sink into the leather seats of my Maserati and start the engine. The drive to Umbria's Universe is quiet, but my head mimics the volume of a concert speaker if I were standing right next to it. Conversation after conversation, memory after memory assaults my mind.

After parking in my spot at the back of the casino, I head inside to my office. There are several of my father's men stationed strategically in the casino, no doubt to watch me and not our customers. I nod to the ones I pass, but don't bother saying a word because I know they won't respond. They never do.

When I reach my destination, I close the door and flip the lock. I don't want to be bothered. At least not until I get my thoughts under control. As I slip into my chair, I allow some of the memories that taunted me on the drive here to take hold.

"Malachi, get a grip," my father shouts. "This is what we do."

Ignoring the tears gathering in my eyes, I lunge forward and shove him into the wall. I lean in so my nose is almost touching his.

"And I was fine with it until now. You've crossed a line by taking her."

Undeterred by my rage, my father spits out, "She was making you soft. There's no room for soft in the Ricci family."

"No, you mean she was making me human." I push away from him and drag my hands over my face. "Of all the people you could have trafficked, all the people who wouldn't be missed, why did it have to be Mina?"

Images blur and shift, carrying me to another memory, the one I've tried to scrub from my gray matter.

"Mal, please, don't let him do this."

I stare at Mina, the woman who owns my heart and soul, and silently beg her to understand. I want to save her, I need to save her, but I can't.

"Mina, I love you."

Her face hardens, and her tears die down. "If you loved me, you'd fix this." She reaches her hand through the bars of the caged room and grips mine. "We can run away together. You'd never have to step foot near him again."

I shake my head. "I can't. You know I can't. If I do that, he'll find us."

"No he won't," Mina insists. "We'll get new identities, leave the country and start over. We can do this, Mal, I know we can."

The more she talks, the longer I look at her beautiful face, the more I want to believe she's right. Maybe we can do this. Maybe my father would give up after a while if we can't be found. Maybe, maybe, maybe.

A knock on my office door pulls me from the scene flashing in my head.

"What?" I bark.

The door opens and Tonya, one of our escorts, slinks in. She's not my favorite person in the world, but she helps keep the others in line, so I keep her around. Tonya is wearing the uniform all the girls wear when they work the casino: black thong bodysuit that shows just as much tits as it does ass, pantyhose, and black stilettos. Her nails are painted blood red and her hair is curled around her face.

I groan. "Whatever it is, Tonya, can it wait?"

She shakes her head and moves to stand beside my chair. I stiffen, and not in a good way. I'm not in the mood for anything she has to offer.

"You look tired," she says as she reaches out to glide a pointed nail over my cheek. "I think I can help with that."

I push her hand aside. "What do you want?"

Tonya squares her shoulders and sighs. "I wanted to let you know that we're probably gonna have to fire Tempe. She's declining all requests for her services and refuses to work the floor tonight."

One doesn't simply get fired from Umbria's Universe, and Tonya knows this. All of our escorts and most of our casino employees are women my father hand selected from our trafficking business to work for us. They are the best of the best when it comes to their physical attributes. Tempe has only been here a few weeks and still has yet to embrace the lifestyle.

"I'll handle it," I tell her.

"With all due respect," she begins. "I think it would be best if—"

"I said I'll handle it," I snap from behind clenched teeth. "Is that all?"

Tonya narrows her eyes at me, but when I return her gaze, she ducks her head. "Yes, that's all."

"Good. You can leave now."

Tonya pauses like she's about to argue, but she must think better of it because she turns and walks out the door, pulling it shut behind her. Alone again, I breathe a sigh of relief and shift my focus to my computer.

I click on the icon to open up the security feeds and check on the casino floor. All the girls, sans Tempe, are hard at work. The customers are feeding the machines as if their lives depend on it. Everything is running smoothly.

I minimize the security window, and after a dozen more clicks, open the secret folders I keep hidden deep in my hard drive.

All of the documentation, *the evidence*, I've been collecting since that last night with Mina stares back at me from the screen. I peruse the files until I find the one I'm looking for, the picture that will remind me of why I have to fight for what I believe in, even if it means taking down my family.

Mina's smile, even only on a computer screen, lights up the room. Her chestnut hair and green eyes suck me in, despite knowing they aren't real. Not anymore. I press a finger to her cheek, imagining my touch warming her skin, lighting a fire that only I was ever able to fuel and extinguish in her.

"I'm trying, Mina." I breathe deeply. "I promise I am."

CHAPTER 5

Harlow

"WHY?" *he rasps.*

"Why what?" I arch a brow as I grip the hem of my tank and pull it over my head. Next, I remove my bra and let it slip from my fingers to fall to the floor.

Malachi's nostrils flare, and his eyes darken to mimic a stormy sea. My hands go to the button on my jeans, ready to free myself of the last remaining barriers to my body. His hungry gaze follows.

"Why do I want you so bad?"

I lift a shoulder, and as I start to push the denim and lace over my hips, he growls. Lunging forward, Malachi grips my wrists to stop my movements and yanks me toward him until my tits press against his chest. My nipples protest against his dress shirt, hardening to tight buds and demanding attention.

"Let me," he growls in my ear as his hands replace mine and he shoves my jeans and panties down.

Malachi bends down and sucks a nipple into his mouth while he rolls and pinches the other between his fingers. I throw my head back on a moan. I lower my own hand to my pussy and press two fingers to my clit. Between the wet heat of his mouth and the friction I'm creating, I'll explode before we even really get started.

And I don't give a fuck.

Malachi releases my nipple with a pop of his lips and drops to his knees. He nips at my fingers and nudges them away with his nose before palming my ass cheeks and pulling me to his mouth. The second his tongue swipes through my folds only to flatten on my clit, my hips buck.

"Mmm," he groans against me, the vibrations threatening to send me over the edge. "Delicious."

He swirls his tongue at an unrelenting pace. He loosens his grip and his fingertips trail over my ass cheeks toward the crease to spread them. Malachi teases my puckered hole and pushes a finger inside up to the first knuckle. When he withdraws it, I whimper.

He chuckles against my core, I expect him to deny me what I want, but he doesn't. He laps at my pussy, increasing the pressure, and reinserts his finger, farther this time. The tingling builds until it's almost unbearable. I fist my hands in his hair to hold on for what promises to be the most explosive—

Footsteps have my eyes shooting open, and I find myself staring at Peppermint. She's standing next to my bed with a giant smirk on her face.

"Must have been some dream," she snarks, nodding at my waist.

I glance down and see my hand between my legs, and I quickly pull it away. My inner slut immediately misses the contact and begs me to keep chasing what she so desperately needs, but the rational side of me shuts her down.

"Well?" Peppermint prods.

"Well what?" I swing my legs over the edge of the mattress and bend down to grab the oversized tee from the floor. I sleep naked, always have, but I always cover up when the chill of the morning air hits my skin.

No chill today. There's nothing but mind-numbing, salacious heat.

"Who were you fucking?"

I shrug. "Don't know."

"The faceless fuck again?" Peppermint shakes her head. "You need to get laid, Har. Like yesterday."

The faceless fuck. It's an apt description for the dreams I've been having since Jack kicked me to the curb. Until last night. Until Malachi. But telling her the truth about who I was dreaming about will surely result in the club having me committed.

"You're one to talk." I immediately regret my words when I see the flash of pain in her eyes. "Sorry, that was uncalled for."

"You're right, it was." Peppermint follows me into the attached bath where I turn on the shower and wait for the water to warm up. "But I forgive you. Besides, you know I'm right."

I slip back out of my tee, questioning my sanity for even putting it on. Habit I suppose. As I step under the spray, Peppermint hops up onto the counter.

"Did you need something, Pep?" I ask.

"Nah." She chuckles. "I just wanted to watch you diddle your skittle."

"Funny." I lather shampoo into my hair and rinse it out. "What did you need?"

Peppermint sighs. "You're no fun, ya know that?"

"But you love me anyway," I retort while I squeeze body wash over my loofah. "So, why'd I wake up to you watching me sleep."

"Brazen called."

"Okay. What'd she want?"

"I don't know. Said she needed to talk to you. I told her I'd have you call her when you got up."

"Jesus, Peppermint," I sputter, trying not to choke on the water running over my face. "When the president of the mother chapter calls, you don't make her wait for a return call."

"Chill out, Har. I told her you were checking on yesterday's rescues." My VP huffs out a breath. "This isn't my first rodeo."

"Right. Sorry."

I seem to be doing that a lot lately. Apologizing to my best friend. Maybe she's right and I need to get laid. Fuck out some of my stress.

Target practice last night was supposed to do that for you.

When I'm clean, I turn the water off and reach out to grab the towel on the rack. Peppermint slides off the counter to her feet. She leaves the bathroom and I follow. Grabbing my cell off my nightstand, she hands it to me.

"Thanks," I say as I sit on the bed, wrapped in a towel.

I pull up Brazen's contact info and tap on it to call her. She answers on the second ring.

"Harley," Brazen says, using my road name. My chapter sisters have always stuck with my given name, unless we're on a rescue mission, but the other chapters all use my road name. "I've got Rebel on with me," she says, referring to her VP.

I hit the speakerphone button. "I've got Peppermint here as well."

"Hey, P," Brazen says. "Sorry I didn't fill you in earlier. Felt it was important to do this all at once."

"It's all good," Peppermint tells her. "I understand."

"When are we taking out your bastard ex, Harley?" Rebel asks, evil glee in her voice.

I laugh, but it's forced. Everyone knows about my break-up, and while I appreciate the support, it's not something I want to hash out or discuss on a regular basis.

"Soon, Rebel."

What I don't say is we're never doing that. Jack might have been an ass for dumping me the way he did, but his reasons were valid. I couldn't give him what he wanted. That's on me… not that I'll admit that out loud.

"Just let me know and we'll be there." That's saying something since the mother chapter is located in Widow's Creek, Kentucky. Not exactly a quick trip.

"Anyway, we need to discuss the Ricci Crime Family," Brazen says, shutting down further conversation that isn't regarding business. "After you filled me in last night, I had one of our sisters do some more digging."

"I have Story digging into it too," I remind her. "She's supposed to give us an update at church tonight."

"Might want to move up that meeting."

I meet Peppermint's eyes over the phone. Her expression is dark.

"I can do that."

"Good, because I've got another mission for you." Brazen takes a deep breath. "Seems the Ricci Crime Family isn't holding up their end of the peace treaty they signed with Velvet."

Pain stabs my heart at the mention of my mom, and my stomach tightens, a ball of dread forming deep in my gut. Peppermint pulls her own cell out of her cut and flips it so I can see her screen fill with the notes app. I nod, silently thanking her for making sure we get all the details.

"Lay it on me, Brazen," I say.

"They're using their escort business as a cover for sex trafficking."

My mind flashes back to my dream, but I squash the image. I knew my attraction for Malachi couldn't go anywhere, but this only hammers home that fact.

"But the treaty," I protest, wanting to believe that she's wrong, that my mom didn't die for no fucking reason. "They signed a fucking contract with us. We all agreed: no more trafficking and we'd stand down from any territory disputes as long as those boundaries were respected."

"Apparently treaties don't mean shit to the Italians."

"Did you get any info on their next exchange?" I ask, trying to keep myself calm.

Hard to do when you just learned that evil has been operating right under your nose and you missed it. Or now that you have to kill the man you were just fantasizing about.

"No, we weren't able to figure that out. I'm hoping Story can find whatever it is we're missing."

"I'll get her on it right away," I assure her. "I can fill you in after we meet."

"Perfect." Brazen pauses, and it's in that span of a few seconds that I realize I'm not going to like what she's going to say next. As if what she's already divulged isn't bad enough. "I want you to go see Malachi."

Panic seizes me. "Why?"

"To try and buy you a little more time. He gave you forty-eight hours. Convince him you're really contemplating his offer. Ask him to give you a week. That will give your chapter a chance to figure out the time of the next exchange and plan a rescue mission that will also result in wiping the Italians out."

"And if he doesn't agree?" I ask, running through all the possibilities in my head.

"Then we go to war."

After assuring Brazen that I'll meet with Malachi, and her promising to have all the intel they gathered sent to Story, we end the call.

"I already sent a text telling everyone to come to the club-house early," Peppermint says before I even have a chance to set my phone down.

"Thanks."

"Har, I don't like waiting."

I lift my head and lock eyes with her. I know she's remembering her time with traffickers, all those years ago, and it breaks my heart that she relives it with every rescue. But that can't be helped, and she gets to take out her tormentors over and over and over again with each kill she makes. I tell myself that's enough, even when I know it doesn't even begin to make things right for her.

And again, there's that pesky little detail about her tormentors still doing as they please.

"I know you don't." I stand and move to my dresser to pull out some clothes. "Honestly, I don't think you'll have to. There's no way Malachi will agree to more time. If we're lucky, the Italians will be a thing of the past by tomorrow night and their victims will be free."

"We should've killed them years ago," Peppermint says vehemently.

"Yeah, we should've. But that's not what happened."

I clench my teeth, remembering how I wanted to go out, guns blazing, and end every last fucker in that stupid family, remembering how I was told to stand down, that my mother wouldn't have wanted a war. I remember how pissed off I was at not being in charge because I was too young, at how helpless I felt when Peppermint sobbed because the people who orchestrated her trauma were going to get away with it.

"We're gonna make this right, Har. Tell me we're gonna make this right."

I grab my cut off the hook by the door and slip it on, then shift back to my dresser and lift my hatchet to hold it in front of me. I lock eyes with Peppermint.

"Yeah, Pep. We're gonna make it right. I promise."

CHAPTER 6

Malachi

IT'S BEEN thirty-six hours since I gave Harlow an ultimatum and nothing has happened. I swallow my disappointment, reminding myself that there's still time.

Not enough.

Pushing up from my office chair, I button my suit jacket and stride out to the casino floor. I like to interact with our customers, stay visible to not only them but my employees as well. As soon as I clear the dollar slot machine area, my head of security comes rushing toward me from the direction of the front entrance.

"Sir, we've got a problem," Gill says.

My eyes dart in the direction he came from, but I see nothing alarming. I swallow a sigh. Gill is the perfect man to head up my security team. He's thorough, vigilant, and doesn't have a problem with getting his hands dirty. On the flip side of that though is a paranoia to rival that of a frat boy who ate too many pot brownies. Gill regards everything as a problem, a threat.

"If it's a customer getting too handsy with the girls, throw 'em out. I don't have time to deal with it." We may be an upscale casino, but we're not immune to lower-class problems.

Gill narrows his eyes at me, his jaw clenched, and I'm reminded why it's a good thing that I'm his boss and not the other way around. His shoulders stiffen and his hands curl into fists at his side.

"You have a visitor, sir."

"And that's a problem because…"

Gill looks over his shoulder for a moment before facing me again and leaning closer. "She's carrying a hatchet, sir," he whispers to keep customers from hearing him.

There's only one person I know who carries a weapon like that, and just picturing her has my dick twitching.

"Well, did you take it from her?" I ask, doing my best to act as if knowing Harlow is close has no effect on me.

Gill's face reddens. "Bitch threatened to cut off my balls if I did. Brought the blade right between my legs."

I manage to contain my laugh because I should be mad at him. But it's not easy.

"I pay you to keep this place secure, Gill."

"Yes, sir."

I decide to let him off the hook… this time.

"Bring her to my office." I turn on my heel but before I get too far, I look over my shoulder and call out to him. "And Gill."

"Sir?"

"She better not have that hatchet on her when I see her."

I smirk to myself and retreat back to my office to wait for him to bring me the little hellcat. After ten minutes, I start to question my order because they still aren't here.

Another five minutes goes by before there's a sharp knock on my door.

"Come in."

The door swings open, and when Gill strides in with his grip around Harlow's bicep, I can't contain my laughter. In front of me is this six-foot five behemoth of a man, nose bloody, a deep gash on his arm, and claw marks on his cheeks. But he's holding the damn hatchet.

Harlow barely clears his pecs, her arms are zip tied behind her back, and she's got marks on her arms that will surely turn to bruises. It's those marks, those dark spots that have my humor washing away under a crushing wave of fury.

He hurt her. And for some reason, that has all of my protective instincts kicking into overdrive, the instincts I thought I'd lost right along with Mina.

Damn witchy woman.

"Thank you, Gill," I say, my voice tight. I want to launch myself over the desk and add to his injuries, but I hold back. He was only following my orders. It's not his fault I'm reacting irrationally. "You can go."

Gill strides forward and sets the hatchet on my desk before leaving my office. I stare at Harlow, who remains near the door, and think about how to play this. Letting her see how angry I am at her injuries is out of the question, but so is revealing the relief I feel that she showed up at all.

"Ya gonna let me out of these things or what?" she asks, shifting sideways to show me her bound hands.

And that's how I'm going to play this.

I lean a hip against my desk and cross my ankles. "I could, but what fun would that be?"

"Dying isn't any fun either," she quips. "So unless you want to meet your maker, you might want to rethink this strategy."

Dropping my stare, I take in her attire: tight jeans, black boots, dark green tank, and her club's signature cut. I take my time and allow myself to really enjoy the sight before me. I slide my hand toward her hatchet and watch the way her eyes blaze green fire, the way her nostrils flare when my fingers wrap around the handle. I can't help but wonder if she'd be this responsive in bed.

Lifting the weapon, I push to stand at my full height and saunter toward her. I expect to see fear, but all I see is hate warring with unsatiated desire and a dash of confusion. Her eyes follow my every move, and when I'm standing chest to chest with her, her breathing stutters.

I lean around her and press my lips to her ear as I cut the zip tie. "I have no interest in death, but I'd be more than happy to introduce you to heaven."

Harlow lets her arms fall to her sides. I cup her neck to hold her in place, waiting for her to pull away, but she doesn't move. Not an inch.

"Mmm, very happy, *bella*," I murmur.

That snaps her out of whatever trance she was in, and she grips the lapels of my jacket to spin me around and pin me to the wall. No small feat considering our difference in sizes. She grabs her hatchet and I let her, not interested in a fight.

"The only thing you could introduce me to is the grimy, sleezy, vile underbelly of Hell."

I jerk out of her hold and straighten my clothes. "You can try to cover up whatever is going on in your panties, but I saw all I needed to see in your eyes. You want me and you fucking hate yourself for it." I step around her to stride toward my desk. "It's going to be very interesting to see which one wins." I turn around and see she's done the same so we're facing one another. "My money is on want." I motion to a chair. "Have a seat."

Harlow stares at me for a long moment before sitting, but she stays on the edge of the chair like she needs to be ready to pounce at any second. I take my seat and relax into the supple leather.

"Put your claws back in," I say. "You came here, remember?"

"You think I want to be here?"

"No, I don't imagine you do." *But one of these days you'll come to me because you can't stand not to.* "I take it you made a decision regarding my offer."

"I need more time," she blurts out.

Not what I was expecting, but not a 'no' so… "And why should I give you what you need?"

Harlow clenches her teeth so hard I'm afraid they'll break right in front of me. "You came to me first, Malachi." She sneers my name, and it irritates me that I don't hate it. "If you really want to buy Devil's Double Down, you'll give me more time to think about it."

"You're seriously considering it?" I ask doubtfully.

She pauses for a split second before nodding. "I am."

That pause, that fraction of a second in time tells me otherwise. "I see. And how much more time are we talking?"

"A week."

"This wouldn't be your way of giving your club time to gear up for a war, would it?"

She turns her hatchet over and over in her hands as she takes a few deep breaths. I hit a nerve, and I know it. But what nerve was it?

"Unlike you and yours, I don't lie. If I say I need more time to think, it's because I need more goddamn time to think. I could easily have shown up here, all of Devil's Handmaidens in tow and started the war you seem hell bent on inciting, but I didn't. I came alone."

I pretend to think about her words. In truth, I don't need to think about a damn thing. If this is all a ruse and her club wants a war, great. That's what I want. Because I need them to do what I can't: take out the trash.

But if she is genuinely considering my offer, that's fine too and my plan B. Because buying a new casino, taking back what my father already deems as ours, will distract enough of the family that I can take out the trash myself. And hopefully, when all is said and done, those remaining will be so pleased with what I'm bringing to the table and not what I took away that I'll have little opposition.

Either way, I win. Either way, I get revenge for Mina.

"Okay," I finally say."

Her eyes lock on mine. "Okay?"

"I'm not an unreasonable man, Harlow. If you say you need more time, I can give you more time."

"I, um, thank you."

This is the first time I've spoken to her and she hasn't seemed confident. I find it a little unnerving. I like her fiery side.

"Is a week sufficient?"

"Yes."

"Done." I rise to my feet. "I'll have Gill escort you out," I say as I grab my cell to send him a text.

Harlow shoots to her feet. "If that goon gets within five feet of me, I'll gut him like I should've earlier," she snaps, lifting her hatchet.

I grin, glad to see the dip in confidence was temporary. "Fair enough."

Harlow walks to the door, pausing with her hand on the knob. "See you in a week."

"I look forward to it, *bella*," I say as she pulls the door open and disappears into the hallway.

Once I'm alone, I scroll through my recent contacts list on my cell until I find the number I want and tap it.

"Please tell me you have good news," he says by way of greeting.

"The bait is set," I tell him, grateful that I'm able to. "It shouldn't be long now."

CHAPTER 7

Harlow

FREEDOM.

That's what being on my Harley gives me. Freedom, peace, a sense of being centered in a world where everything around me is spinning chaotically into the eye of a tornado. Normally, I can climb on my matte black bike, with its chrome accents, and the vibrations lull me into a calm headspace.

Not today though. My brain is swirling with turmoil, the past, present, and future creating the perfect seemingly insurmountable storm.

When I left Umbria's Universe I fully intended to go to the clubhouse and meet with my officers to see what, if any, additional information they've obtained on the Ricci's. After church yesterday, we were all in agreement that we take this week to prepare for war. If the Italians want to break the treaty, then so be it. But they aren't going to get away with it.

Instead, I found myself at a liquor store buying the fifth of tequila now stashed in my saddlebag and making my way to a strand of beach that's rarely busy. I clear the city, and open up the throttle, letting the sting of the salty ocean air whip at my face. When I reach my turnoff, I take it, only slowing down so I don't get sand in my teeth.

All the while, I'm thinking of *him*. Malachi fucking Ricci. I went to see him as instructed and everything went according to plan. Well, if you don't count the little tiff with his security goon. Even still, I left feeling like it was too easy. Like there's something I'm missing, something that changes everything.

And then there's the way his touch seared my flesh, the way my pussy wept when he broke contact with me and put distance between us. I shouldn't want him, *crave* him, but for reasons I don't understand, I do. *Desperately*. Something tells me he'd be dynamite in bed.

But it would be futile to give in to my baser instincts. Nothing could ever come of it, and I've never been the type of bitch to fuck and flee. Damn feelings get in the way. Feelings that I can't put voice to, which only ends with me being emotionally fractured.

After parking my bike, I walk over the small dune, liquor bottle in hand, and breathe a sigh of relief when I see the stretch of beach is empty. No need for anyone to see my impending meltdown.

I slump to the ground and draw my knees up to my chest as I unscrew the bottle cap and take a giant swig. The liquid burns a path to my belly, and I savor it, letting it fill all of my empty spaces.

Tipping my head back, I raise the bottle in the air. "This is for you, Mom. And all the ones we couldn't save, the ones I know you're taking care of now."

I swallow a few more gulps and let my mind wander.

"Can you at least tell me where you're going?" I ask my mom, fearing I'll get the same stock answer I always do.

"To take out the fuckers we rescued them from," she says coldly, swinging her arm to indicate the room.

I watch her go, but when the sun bursts through the opening exit door, I call out to her.

"I love—"

The door slams shut in her and Tahiti's wake.

You.

Panic squeezes its pain studded fist around my heart. My mother and I have never left one another without saying I love you to each other. Never.

I turn back to the girl my mom promised safety to. She's curled on her side, staring at the door, same as I was, a forlorn look on her face.

"What's your name?" *I ask her.*

She flips to her other side, and her eyes find mine as her bottom lip quivers. There's an IV attached to the back of her hand and the pole is on the opposite side of the cot I'm standing on. She appears to be about my age, but it's hard to tell with the dirt caking her face and blanket covering her body.

"Pepper," *she finally responds, her voice breaking.*

I sit down on the floor next to her cot. "I'm Harlow. And that was my mom, Velvet."

Pepper nods before darting her eyes around the large under-ground space. "Why did she leave?"

"Club business," *I say automatically. When Pepper's brow wrinkles in confusion, I don't bother trying to explain. Besides, I can't explain what I don't really understand myself. I thought I did… until this.* "Do you have family?" *I ask her in an attempt to divert the conversation.*

Pain fills Pepper's eyes, and her shoulders shake with sobs. She opens her mouth to speak, but nothing comes out save her crying. Finally, she nods.

I reach out intent on grabbing her hand but hesitate before making contact. I'm not one to give comfort. I don't know how to do this. But my mom asked me to do this for a reason, so dammit, I'm going to.

Taking a deep breath, I wrap my hand around Pepper's, gently so as not to hurt her. Her eyes widen for a second and then the dam she's so desperately trying to keep in place breaks, and she wails. Her cries seem to set off a domino effect on the others, and the sound in the room intensifies. I even shed a few tears myself for these people I don't know, for their obvious pain.

I don't know how long I sit there with Pepper, but it doesn't matter. I'd sit here for as long as I have to. Because I said I would. I roam my gaze over the room every few minutes, making sure that the others are being taken care of. They are. And I knew they would be. The Devil's Handmaidens are making sure of it.

At some point, I must doze off because the next thing I know, I'm batting my eyelids at being woken up by a hand shaking my shoulder.

Mom's back!

I peer at Pepper and assure myself she's asleep before slipping my hand from hers and scrambling to my feet. I whirl around to throw my arms around my mom but freeze when I see it's Tahiti.

Her face is bloody, her clothes are torn, and she has several gashes on her arms that will likely need stitches. But it's the look on her face that has me frantically shaking my head, it's the tears in her eyes that have me turning in circles searching for my mom. It's the utter devastation coming off of Tahiti in waves that tells me everything I need to know.

Mom isn't here. And she never will be again.

I take another few gulps of the tequila as the memory shifts.

"How?" I demand as I throw my hatchet at one of the targets set up outside the clubhouse, a couple floodlights on so I can see in the dark. "It's been two fucking days, and no one will tell me what the fuck happened."

I stride forward to yank my weapon out of the thick slab of wood and trudge back to the throwing line. I've been at it for hours, my mind begging my body for exhaustion. I know I should stop, try to get some sleep, but I can't. The funeral is tomorrow, and I can't bear the thought of burying my mom when I don't even know how the hell she died.

"Har, it's club bu—"

I whirl on Tahiti, lifting my hatchet above my head like I'm getting ready to swing on her. "Don't you dare tell me it's club business!" I shout, tears blurring my vision. "She's my fucking mom. I deserve to know." I swipe my arm across my face to wipe away the flowing tears. "One minute she was there and the next…"

Tahiti looks away for a moment, and her chest rises and falls with her deep breaths. When her eyes find mine, the anguish I see in their depths only amplifies my own. Tahiti loved my mom, same as I did. She's hurting too and I hate that I'm making it worse, but I can't help it.

I lower my arm and fall to my knees, the hatchet coming to rest next to me. For several minutes, the only sound is erratic heartbeat throbbing in my ears and the occasional sniffle from crying.

Tahiti is silent too… until she's not.

"She gave herself up."

My head whips up and then I rub my nose on my sleeve. "What?" I ask, sure I heard her wrong.

Tahiti lowers to the ground, sitting across from me. She's staring, but not at me. Her eyes are focused on something beyond me, something I imagine isn't really there.

She takes a deep breath and starts talking. "We went back to the last known location of the traffickers. We weren't able to take them all out initially, so we had to go back. I don't think any of us thought there'd still be people lingering, not after the bloodshed of that morning, but we were wrong." Tahiti runs a hand through her hair but still doesn't look at me. "Fuck, we were so wrong. Not only were the ones we missed still there, but they had reinforcements."

I listen to Tahiti so intently, someone could be screaming 'fire' through a bullhorn directly into my ear and I wouldn't notice. I'm hanging on her every word.

She swallows before continuing. "I don't know if they knew we'd be back or if someone tipped them off." Tahiti shrugs. "That's not something we'll ever know, I guess. But when Velvet saw how many of those Italian fuckers we'd have to go up against, with only four of us, she changed the plan."

"And you let her?" I ask.

Tahiti lets out a humorless chuckle. "You know how Velvet was. Once her mind was made up, there was no stopping her." Finally, her eyes meet mine. "Anyway, she put her weapons down and started walking right in the line of fire with her hands raised so they'd see she wasn't a threat. I yelled at her to stop, but she didn't listen. And I kept expecting to see my best friend gunned down, but miraculously, she wasn't. Instead, a man started walking toward her, his arms raised."

I try to picture the scene, imagine my mom walking straight toward her death, but it's impossible. My mom is—was—invincible. And she wasn't stupid.

"What happened next?" I ask, not wanting to know but also needing to at the same time.

"We had our comms in, so we could hear everything that was being said. Velvet introduced herself to the man, who we now know was Antonio Ricci. She said she wanted to call a truce, but she had conditions."

"She wouldn't do that," I insist.

"But she did, Har. She would and she did." Tahiti takes another deep breath. "Ricci laughed at her, at first. Couldn't understand what made her think he would ever call a truce, but she convinced him. Said that she wanted a signed peace treaty to assure the club that the Ricci's would stop sex trafficking and to make clear that DHMC and the Ricci Crime Family had to exist in the same territory, but that they would never interfere with one another's businesses."

I shake my head. "But that doesn't make sense. I wouldn't have agreed to that if I were him. He doesn't get shit out of it."

"That's what he said. But there was one thing no one was counting on."

"What?"

"You're mom's understanding that sometimes a person just needs revenge to feel like they're coming out the winner."

"I don't understand."

"When we did the initial rescue, we killed several of Ricci's men.

One of those men was his youngest son, Mortichi. Velvet knew this and told Ricci that he could take her life once the treaty was signed. He immediately agreed."

Tahiti reaches into the inside pocket of her cut and pulls out an envelope. Bloody fingerprints are smudged on the paper, and when she hands it to me, I recoil, shaking my head. She sets it on the ground next to my hatchet then gets to her feet.

I hear the flick of a Zippo coming to life and smell the smoke from Tahiti's cigarette. I look up and focus on the orange glow of the cherry.

"They let me talk to her for a minute before… well, before."

A whimper escapes me, but I stop it with a hand over my mouth.

"She, uh…" Tahiti takes a drag of her smoke and exhales. "She loved you, Har. So fucking much. She did this for you, so you would live in a world that had a little less evil in it. The Ricci Crime Family still exists, but they won't be hurting any more innocent people."

Her boots crunching over twigs as she walks away barely register. And when I'm sure I'm alone, I throw my head back and scream until my throat hurts. I scream until there's no noise left in me. I scream until exhaustion takes over and my brain can no longer give my body commands.

As the memory recedes, the sun is setting over the horizon. I grip the tequila bottle and bring it to my lips. Nothing comes out when I tip it back, so I throw it as hard as I can, wishing like hell I could hear the satisfying shatter of glass instead of the muted thump on sand.

I try to stand, but the alcohol makes it impossible, and I fall back down on my ass. And just like ten years ago, I throw my head back and scream until exhaustion wins out.

CHAPTER 8
Malachi

TODAY HAS BEEN a day from hell. If it could go wrong, it did. I slept through my alarm, so I was late to the casino. Then I had to 'handle' Tempe because she was still refusing to work. I would've had Gill handle it, but my father ordered me to do it. Everyone thinks she's a pile of ash, incinerated by the mortician on the family's payroll, but in reality, she's on a bus headed to who the fuck knows where with the twenty grand in cash and the new identity I gave her to start fresh.

As if that weren't enough, I had to give myself injuries to make it look like she put up a fight. When I get home, I need to clean my raw knuckles and any other scrapes and cuts I gave myself, and put an ice pack on the growing lump on the side of my head. Then there's the matter of my ruined clothes because I had to make it look like I actually did dirty work. Those are going straight into the trash.

I probably went overboard when I punched that tree, so many times I lost count, and then slammed my head into it for good measure. To say I've been on edge since Harlow walked out of my office two days ago would be an understatement. I suppose all my pent-up frustration and sexual tension fueled my actions earlier.

After parking my car, which now needs to be detailed thanks to my dirty clothes, in my garage, I slip into the house through the door leading to the kitchen. I strip naked, toss all the garments in the garbage can, and head to the attached bath in the master suite.

Bracing myself with my palms flat against the tile, I watch as crimson water swirls down the shower drain and hiss at the stinging of my injuries. Once the water runs clear, I straighten to wash my hair.

And my mind clouds with images of a certain biker chick, naked and writhing beneath me. Lathered shampoo forgotten, I let the fantasy take shape and imagine Harlow spread out on my silk sheets, pussy on full display, nipples pebbled, begging to be pinched.

Wrapping my hand around my cock, my body demands my brain to register it as Harlow's tight cunt surrounding me. I plunge into her wet heat, over and over again, my hips pistoning back and forth. I can hear her moaning my name, begging me to come inside of her, pleading with me to give her the release she knows only I can give.

I tighten my grip to mimic the feel of her walls spasming around me and pump harder. One pump, two pumps, three.

"Fuuuuuck!" I roar as my orgasm pulses out of my length.

Gasping for breath, I rest my forehead against the tile. Disgust slams into me at having been reduced to an imaginary fuck, but my flaccid dick and loosening muscles are screaming 'thank you'.

I finish up in the shower and quickly dry off. I tend to the scrapes and cuts before striding out into my bedroom to find clean sweats to throw on.

"Ya know we have girls for that."

With my hands in a dresser drawer, my spine stiffens. I close my eyes and silently count to ten before pulling on the sweatpants and turning to face the intruder.

"What are you doing here, Nicholi?" I ask, glaring at my cousin.

I don't give a damn that he heard me having an orgasm to rival all orgasms. I don't care that he saw me naked. Hell, we used to be close, practically brothers, until it all went to shit.

What I do care about is that he's in my home, uninvited. I care that he's sitting in my bedroom, of all places, in the dark, like a damn creep. Or like I'm one of the unlucky individuals on his hit list.

"You wound me, cousin," he says, bringing his hand to rest over his heart… or at least to the space it should be. "I didn't think I needed an invitation to come see you."

"Cut the dramatics," I snap, arms crossed over my chest. "Why are you here?"

Nicholi tilts his head and grins. For a moment, I'm transported back in time to when we were kids. There were four of us Ricci boys, all born into a family we didn't choose: Nicholi and his twin, Nico, and me and my younger brother, Mortichi. Every summer our families would vacation together and the four of us would run wild, all grins and little boy shenanigans.

Those were the days.

"I'll answer your question if you'll answer one for me," he says, pulling me from my thoughts.

"Will that get you the fuck out of my house quicker?"

"Sure."

"Fine." I walk out of the bedroom, knowing he'll follow. If I'm going to have to deal with Nicholi, there's no way I'm doing it without liquor.

When I reach the kitchen, Nicholi's footsteps echoing on the hardwood directly behind me, I get a tumbler and a bottle of whiskey. I pour myself a healthy glass and then turn to face him.

"I'd love a drink, thanks," he says, his expression telling

me he's pleased with himself for getting under my skin. He knows I don't drink whiskey unless I'm pissed.

"You won't be here long enough to enjoy it."

Nicholi's ears redden, the only sign that he's getting angry, and he stalks past me to pour his own drink. I let him do it. Not because I want to, but because this is what Nicholi does. He uses his hulk-like stature and overbearing presence to intimidate people. And I've learned that the more he thinks he's controlling the situation, the less control he actually has.

When he finishes his drink in one gulp, he slams the tumbler on the counter, shattering the glass. Again, I say nothing, react in no visible way. On the inside, however, I'm seething. That was one of a set of six very expensive crystal tumblers.

Bastard.

"Who were you picturing when you were yanking your pecker?" Nicholi asks.

I arch a brow. "Seriously? That's your question?"

He lifts a shoulder. "Humor me."

"No one."

"Bullshit." Nicholi leans against the counter and we're face to face. He's only an inch or two taller than me, but he's wider, bulkier. I can't find it in me to fear him though. "C'mon, cousin, who's cunt were you pretending to bury yourself in? Must've been some prime pussy with the way you screamed there at the end."

And this is why Nicholi will never be fit for polite society. It's why he's the cousin whose job it is to smash faces and take lives. He's the Ricci cousin who fell in line with the family, who never questions an order. I used to be like that, before Mina. Mortichi was a lot like him, too, and I couldn't save my younger brother. I have no desire to even try with Nicholi.

"Fine, I was picturing Candice," I lie, giving him the name of a girl I dated a few years back.

"Oh man, sweet Candy." His lips lift into a smile. "I had her once, ya know? She was primo, cousin."

All I feel is pity. Not for me, not for my cousin, but for Candice. She was a good girl, a sweet girl. There's no telling what happened to her after Nicholi got his hands on her.

"I answered your question. Now answer mine," I demand, getting tired of being in his presence.

He feigns confusion. "What was your question again?"

"Why. Are. You. Here?"

Nicholi snaps his fingers. Fucking prick. "Oh, right." He pushes off the counter. "Uncle Angelo sent me."

"Why?"

"Wanted me to find out how your meeting with that biker bitch went."

My blood boils at his description of Harlow. It doesn't surprise me that my father found out about her visit, not with the amount of his own people he has stashed at the casino. It does surprise me, however, that it took him two days to send Nicholi. He's slipping, which is good.

"Did you start a war or what?" he asks when I don't say anything.

I shake my head. "Not yet. She asked for more time to consider my offer."

"I still don't get why you made the offer in the first place," he complains.

"It was a business decision. You wouldn't understand."

Which is true. It was a business decision. Just not in the way he thinks. And he wouldn't understand. Nicholi is all brawn, no brains.

"Try me," he demands, his ears getting red.

I gulp down my whiskey and pour myself another before answering him.

"It's a numbers game, Nicholi. We make bank with one casino, imagine what we could do with two. Besides, it's better for the family if we have total control of the city. And not because of some fucking treaty signed ten years ago out of some misguided need for revenge."

"Mortichi was your brother," he snarls. "You think Uncle Antonio should've ignored his death, slinked back into a corner and let that bitch get away with killing him?"

"It was Father's fault he was there in the first place," I shout, angry for even having to think about this. That was a bad day for all involved and just because there was no love lost between me and my brother doesn't mean I wanted to see him gunned down. "He got his revenge, sure, but at what cost? We've been bound by a goddamn piece of paper for a decade. I've sat back and played the good Capo, followed the rules and built an empire with Umbria's Universe. And I've done it all with restrictions my father had placed on me. I'm done playing nice. I want more!"

By the time I stop talking, my chest is heaving, and my head is starting to pound. And Nicholi's eyes are lit up with approval.

He claps me on the shoulder as he steps around me toward the front door.

"'Bout time, cousin. I was wondering when you'd finally rejoin the ranks of the ruthless." He pauses with his hand on the doorknob and looks over his shoulder. "And just in time, too. Because the war starts in seventy-two hours."

I slump back against the counter once the door shuts behind him.

Seventy-two hours? I gave Harlow an extra week, hoping the DHMC would start the war. But if my family starts it, she and her club won't stand a chance. There's no way anyone can go up against my family once they have the upper hand. And they will have it.

Scenarios play through my mind on ways to fix this, how to force Harlow's hand without telling her the truth, without divulging the real reason I broke the treaty and without giving up control of the situation. I'm a leader, not a follower.

This was all planned. We made sure of that. But it's falling apart. We didn't prepare for this.

All of that is a hard pill to swallow for two reasons. The first being that I'm going to be forced to admit we need help instead of orchestrating a way to get it without asking. And the second reason?

That's a little more complicated.

Because I find that I want to go to Harlow, to tell her the truth. She stirs something in me that has been dormant for too long, and I want to explore it. I just need to figure out how to do that without her killing me first.

Yeah, complicated as fuck.

CHAPTER 9
Harlow

"GET THEM TO THE VAN!"

I don't bother to make sure my order is followed. It will be. Instead, I race down the tiny hallway to find my prey. I use my hatchet to hack my way through the flimsy door the pasty motherfucker barricaded himself behind.

"Need help?" Spooks asks as she steps up behind me.

I spare her a glance and see Mama standing next to her.

"Nah, just get the girls in the van and make sure they're okay. I'm sure Peppermint and Giggles are fine in the other trailer."

Mama runs to do my bidding, but Spooks remains.

"I bought them, fair and square," the junkie cries out from his hidey hole.

When we arrived at the makeshift campsite, we were greeted by shotgun blasts from one trailer while the other remained unprotected, or so we thought. Mama took out the shooter, and Giggles and Peppermint went to search that trailer. Mama, Spooks and I stormed this one.

A man had been lying on the couch, half naked with a needle still sticking out of his arm. I slit his throat. It wasn't hard to find the two girls we were hired to retrieve after that. They had been wrapped around each other like spider monkeys in the bathtub, having gone there when they heard the gunshots.

We'd gotten the call late last night, the one we all live for. It was the frantic mother of two girls, eleven and nine. She came home from her second shift as an ER nurse to a note from her husband, a recovering addict and the girls' stepfather, telling her he was leaving her. She'd gone into her daughter's room to check on them and both beds were empty, save for another note.

Her husband sold her children to these junkies for his next fix. I don't know if he's thinking she'll thank him for pointing her in the right direction or if, for a brief moment in time, he actually had a conscience, but that note gave us a place to start looking. It took all day, but we're here now and that's what matters.

Based on the condition of the trailers, these sleaze balls were going to pimp the girls out to feed their own habits.

Same story, different family. It happens more than people think, and it disgusts me.

I swing my hatchet one last time, and the wood splinters open, spraying inward toward the pedophile prick. He's cowered in the corner, sniffling like a little bitch.

"Fuck, Prez, you smell that?" Spooks asks, waving her hand in front of her nose. "I think he pissed himself."

"Those girls are mine," he whines.

"Really? Because I thought they belonged to the mother who hired us."

I stride toward him casually, Spooks at my side.

"I paid for them," he says, almost pulling off an indignant tone. Judging by his blown pupils, he's high as a kite. The track marks on his arms tell me he's likely always high as a goddamn kite. "Good money, too."

I tilt my head. "Oh yeah. How much?"

His eyes widen, not in shock, but more like he truly believes we care, like he's proud of himself.

"Five grams of coke for the younger one and four grams for the other."

"Did ya hear that, Spooks?" I ask, conversationally. "A whole nine grams of coke for two little girls. He really broke the bank on that, huh? That's what, close to twenty-five hundred bucks around here?"

"Somewhere in that neighborhood," she confirms.

"And what do you think the value of those girls' lives are, to their mother?"

Spooks whistles. "Wow, that's a hard one." She snakes out her hand and grabs the guy by his stringy hair to haul him to his feet. "I'm gonna guess they're priceless."

I lock eyes with the asshole and nod. "Did ya hear that? Priceless."

He tries to nod but can't with Spooks' grip.

Pressing the tip of my hatchet blade to his thumping carotid, I break the skin and watch as blood trickles out. "Use your words."

"Y-yes. I heard her."

"Good." I pull the blade away and turn my head to look at Spooks. With a smile, I ask, "Now, what do we do to people who pay good money for quality product?"

Referring to this situation in those terms is like swallowing a bowl full of hornets, but it sure is fun to watch our prey squirm with uncertainty, never fully knowing if we're okay with their choices or not.

"Well, most places would reward them." She grins at the man. "You were making a solid investment into your future, right?"

"R-right." His eyes are wide, full of misguided hope.

It's a beautiful sight.

"Then yeah, we should reward him."

"I couldn't agree more," I say and slash my blade across his throat.

Spooks lets him fall to the floor and then kicks him for good measure. I shake my head at her. She loves getting in the last blow, whether it's delivered to a corpse or not.

"Feel better?" I ask, wiping the blood from my hatchet on my jeans and sheathing it.

"Much."

"Me too."

I walk out of the room and out of the trailer, Spooks at my heels. Peppermint is standing next to the van, and Mama is on her Harley. Giggles is in the back with the girls.

"Dammit, I missed all the fun," my VP jokes.

"You also missed the smell of piss, so count yourself lucky," I quip. I jut my chin toward the van. "They okay?"

"Would you be?" she counters and kicks the dirt with the toe of her boot. "They're eleven and nine, Har. Fucking babies."

"And that's my cue to be on my way," Spooks says, mounting her bike. "See ya back at the clubhouse."

"Call their mom and have her meet us at the clubhouse," I instruct her.

"I still don't understand why we don't take them straight to their house. The less people on our property, the better," Spooks grumbles.

"That mother isn't telling a soul about us. We just saved her children. We can trust her."

She nods and tears out of the clearing toward the road. I don't know Spooks' full story, but she has issues. Someday, I hope she trusts us all enough to let us in completely. I know she knows we have her back, will go to battle with her and give our lives for her if need be, but with anything other than that, she's guarded.

I return my attention to my best friend. "Wanna blow shit up?"

Peppermint's face lights up, her upset about the girls temporarily forgotten. Ten minutes later, I watch the flames kiss the sky in my side mirror as I ride away from the site.

The ride back to the clubhouse is calming, quiet in a way that lets my mind rest for the first time in days. The van is parked out front, and it's empty. I smile. Tonight was a good night. I'm so into my post-killing high that I don't even question the car parked next to the van, just assuming it belongs to the girls' mother.

CHAPTER 10

Malachi

A SINGLE HEADLIGHT blinds me from my rearview mirror. I glance at the time on the dash and see it's almost ten o'clock. When I arrived, I was prepared for it to be difficult to gain entry to the DHMC property, but it wasn't. The bobble-headed blonde who was working the gate barely looked at me, and when I told her I had a meeting with Harlow about club business, she waved me in.

I really need to tell Harlow she needs to be more diligent about who she uses for security.

Right, because that will go over well.

I thought for sure that ginger bitch, Peppermint, would have recognized me when she parked next to me in that van, but she was so focused on the vehicle's other occupants that she didn't even notice me.

I watch as Harlow parks her bike and strides toward the cinder block structure I've been told is her clubhouse. In the light shining outside the door, I catch sight of the blood covering her jeans. My hands tighten around the steering wheel, and my stomach flip-flops. Did someone hurt her?

I'll kill 'em.

She's not your problem.

But no matter how many times I tell myself that, I keep coming back to the same thing. I'll fucking murder any person who dares to lay a finger on her, anyone who causes her pain of any kind. I'll savor the way they beg for mercy and then show them none.

She's mine.

It's ironic really, the lengths I'm willing to go for a woman who despises me, a woman I barely know. My father would be proud. He'd tell me I've finally got that Ricci spirit. He should've been proud before, when I tried to stand up for Mina. But even I recognize the difference between then and now.

Back then, I wasn't willing to kill for Mina. I loved her, yes, but I wouldn't have killed for her. I wouldn't have sacrificed my life for hers. I didn't. But I'm willing to now.

For both of them. Mina and Harlow. I'll kill for them both. I'll die for one and kill for both.

It's a cruel realization and a horrible time to have it.

But it changes nothing.

I wait a few more minutes before grabbing the manilla envelope I brought off the passenger seat and leaving the comfort of my Maserati to head into the den of hatred I'm sure will greet me. There's a faint sound of music, but otherwise, it's quiet outside.

The quiet ends as soon as I open the door and step inside. My gaze swings from side to side in an attempt to take in the scene. There's a bar on one side of the room, several women drinking and laughing, seemingly having a good time. The rest of the room is filled with tables and a few couches. A large flat screen TV is mounted on the wall, but it's turned off. There's also a pool table and several dart boards lining the walls.

The entire room is painted black, with a logo of some kind painted on the floor, with a matching one behind the bar.

But none of that registers as crazy. No, what's crazy is that there are children here. Three of them to be exact. A little boy is sitting on a stool behind the bar, talking to a woman I recognize from over the years. Tahiti I think I've heard her called. And two little girls are in the arms of the only woman in the place not wearing a cut.

It's loud, chaotic, and a mixture of badass with a dash of homey. It's not flashy, or even hinting at the wealth I know the club has from their businesses.

I like it.

No one seems to notice me as they continue about their business, but all of that changes when the woman with the little boy behind the bar looks in my direction. She sticks two fingers in her mouth and whistles shrilly.

Suddenly, guns and blades of all kinds are drawn, all pointing at me.

Den of hatred, just like I expected.

Harlow steps away from the woman with the two girls, her hatchet raised above her head. She walks toward me, and the closer she gets, the more uncomfortable my dick becomes tucked in my pants.

"You really do have a fucking death wish, don't you Ricci?" she snarls.

"I thought I told you that death isn't anything I'm interested in," I retort.

Harlow is standing within two feet of me, and I can see her nostrils flare at my reminder of my comment the other day. I still stand by the fact that I'm willing to take her to heaven, but I refrain from saying so. I value my life, despite my actions saying otherwise.

"How did you get in here?"

I tilt my head. "You really should be more diligent about who you let protect your property."

"What's that supposed to mean?"

"It means, the idiot you have stationed at your gate didn't bother checking my story. I told her I had a meeting with you, and she waved me right in. Do you have any idea how dangerous that is if I had truly meant you harm?"

"Peppermint, Giggles," she calls without taking her eyes off of me. "Go *relieve* Trixie of her duties. Remind her what will happen if she steps foot on our property again. And get that prospect patch back. Vinnie, you're on gate duty. Go get whatever shit Trix has in the prospect room and take it out to her."

"On it."

"You got it."

Sure thing, Prez."

Three women rush to do her bidding, only taking their eyes off me when they disperse. Interesting. Harlow commands respect, demands it, and she gets it, no questions asked. One more thing to like about her.

And still not enough to justify the possessiveness you feel toward her.

"What do you want, Ricci?"

I give a slight shake to the manilla envelope. "We need to talk."

She closes the distance between us and presses the tip of the hatchet blade to my chest. "I have nothing to say to you."

"You don't have to say a word. I've got plenty for the both of us."

"Then save it until my week is up. We can talk then."

"That's just it. I can't give you that full week."

Harlow's eyes narrow. "First you go against the treaty, now you're going back on your word. You really don't know shit about loyalty or how to be a decent human being, do you?"

My body goes rigid at her gross misjudgment of me. That's *exactly* why I'm doing what I'm doing, because I'm loyal and decent. I silently count to ten as I remind myself that Harlow doesn't know me, has no clue about my motives for doing what I'm doing.

Yes, I broke the treaty, although I wasn't the first to do so. And yes, I'm going back on my word to give her more time. But I'm doing it because there's no other choice. Sometimes, you have to break a few rules, cross a few lines in order to get to the gold at the end of the proverbial fucking rainbow.

I take a deep breath and force my body to relax. She may not know me now, but she will. I'll take pleasure in introducing her to the man behind her fictitious evil curtain. And that introduction begins right now.

Ignoring the hatchet and the sting of pain my action causes me, I lean forward and growl, "How's this for being a decent human being? In less than forty-eight hours, the Ricci Crime Family, *my* family, is going to start the war *you* wanted more time to prepare for."

CHAPTER 11

Harlow

"DID YOU HEAR ME, *BELLA*?"

Oh I heard him all right. Over and over again, I'm hearing what he said, as if I pushed repeat on my favorite song. Only this isn't my favorite song. Fuck, it's not even my favorite genre of music.

"Why are you telling me this?" I finally find the presence of mind to ask.

Malachi Ricci flusters me, way more than I care to admit. Add in what he just said, and my mind is floating in outer space somewhere.

He shifts his eyes away from mine and looks around the room. I know what he's seeing. Weapons all aimed at him, death glares from my sisters. Most would run the other way when faced with my club, but not him. Not Malachi. He stands here, seemingly cool as can be, like this is just another day at the office.

In fact, not once has he seemed ruffled by me or the club. It's kinda hot.

No. No, no, no.

When his eyes return to lock on mine, there's a determination in them that I'm coming to recognize. He always seems determined, like he's hell bent on getting his way, no matter what it takes.

"Maybe we should go somewhere more private and talk," he suggests.

"Anything you have to say to Prez, you can say to all of us," Mama says as she steps up to my side.

Malachi's gaze bounces between her and me, but it's her he finally focuses on. "All due respect, I don't fucking think so."

I can feel the rage rolling off Mama, and unless I want a full-blown riot, in front of clients and children, no less, I need to cool the situation down. Speaking of clients and children…

"Mama, go get Noah settled in the lounge upstairs."

Mama does as she's told. I hear Noah's protests, his 'aw, do I have to leave', but I ignore it. He's used to hanging out here when he has to. I narrow my eyes at Malachi.

"You, go sit over there," I order, removing my hatchet from his chest and pointing it toward a table in the corner. "I've got something to handle and then we can talk."

He looks like he's going to argue, I expect it, but he doesn't. Instead, he nods.

"You'll sit there and not say a word, got it?"

His lips twitch. "Got it."

I follow his movements until he's seated at the table. Then, and only then, do I face the rest of the room.

"Lower your weapons," I command. "Tahiti, close up shop for the night. Shut everything down. Everyone else, take the next hour and do what you have to so you can stay here for the foreseeable future. We're on partial lockdown until further notice. You better be back here in one hour. We'll have church then. If you're not, there will be hell to pay."

"What about the casino?" one of the more recent rescues asks.

"I'll call Fox," I say, referring to another patched member. "She's running the show over there and knows what to do."

My sisters scramble to do as they're told. I spare a glance at Malachi as I sheath my hatchet and see that he's watching me, intently. I wish I knew what he was thinking.

I walk to the mother and two little girls, who are huddled against a wall, where they retreated to when Malachi walked in and my club reacted. Crouching down to eye level, I smile.

"I'm really sorry about all of that," I say. "It can get a little crazy around here."

The mother looks worried, and I hate that. And the girls? Their fear is palpable.

"Is everything okay?" the mother asks.

I keep my smile in place. "Of course."

She appears relieved and kisses the top of both her daughters' heads. "Okay. We'll get out of your way, then. Seems like you've got some things to take care of."

"I do, but you don't have to rush off."

I need them to leave, but the last twenty-four hours have been traumatic for them so what they need takes priority.

"No, we do. I want to get on the road. We're going to stay with my folks for a while." Her eyes brim with tears. "I can't thank you enough for everything. If I'd lost them, I don't—"

"Don't go there," I tell her softly. "You're all together and that's what matters. I would recommend that they talk to someone. It's going to be a long road for you all, but you'll come out the other side stronger."

"Thank you again."

"You're very welcome."

The mother stands and ushers the girls toward the door. Before they leave, the nine-year-old breaks away and rushes back to me, throwing her arms around my waist. Her little body is dirty, shaking, but her hold is so strong.

"Thanks for coming to get us." Her voice is small, scared, and shaky.

"Anytime."

After the three of them are gone, I simply stand there,

staring at the closed door, and try to soak up the good that came from this night. A family reunited, two children safe, three fuckers dead. A lot of damn good.

I heave a sigh. Why, then, do I feel nothing but dread?

The man sitting in the corner booth comes to mind. Unable to put this off any longer, I spin and cross the room. Once I'm standing in front of him, I force the entire day to wash away so I can focus on why he's here, what he has to say.

"Follow me," I say.

I head in the direction of my office, not bothering to see if he actually follows. He will. When I reach my office, I unlock the door and go in, stepping to the side to wait on him.

Two seconds later, he enters, swinging his head to look for me when he sees I'm not at my desk. I push the door shut behind him and take a step toward my desk.

Fingers wrap around my bicep, and I'm spun around and pinned against the closed door. I see Malachi's eyes, dark and brooding, a millisecond before his mouth crashes against mine. I stiffen and press my hands against his chest, but when his tongue darts out and traces the seam of my lips, I surrender.

What was meant to be me pushing him away turns into me gripping the lapels of his always present suit jacket and tugging him closer. This kiss… holy fuck, this kiss. Malachi tastes like wintergreen and bad decisions, with the slightest hint of whiskey.

I slant my head to deepen the kiss and Malachi moves his hands from the wall beside my head to rest on my hips. His fingers dig into my flesh though my clothes, but I want to feel them, feel *him*, skin to skin.

All rational thought is gone in the absolute primal clash of mouths. Every single reason why this is wrong disappears into the stratosphere. The undeniable hatred I have for this man and what he does ceases to exist.

The only thing that matters in this moment is Malachi and me, his body and my body, our individual needs to use each other to erase whatever is torturing our souls. Him and me. Cock and pussy. Complete and total obliteration.

I break the kiss to shed my cut and rip my shirt over my head. Malachi's eyes dip to the dark green lace of my bra, where they remain fixated while he unbuttons my jeans and shoves them over my hips to pool at my feet.

He takes a step back and peruses my body, head to toe, inhaling sharply when he's done.

"Fuck me, Ricci," I demand, although it comes out more as a plea.

His eyes snap to mine. "Malachi," he snaps. "To you, I'm Malachi. Say it, *bella*. Let me hear my name on your lips."

If I wasn't on fire before, I am now. A blazing inferno is spreading through my veins.

"Malachi."

He leans in and presses his lips to my ear. "That's right, Harlow." He trails his tongue along the lobe. "Tell me what you want," he whispers.

There's a part of me that hates him even more for what he's doing to me, for the responses he's eliciting from my body. But I'm too far into this to care. There will be plenty of time for hate and regret later.

"I need you to fuck me."

Malachi pulls back to stare into my eyes. "Need or want?" he asks as his hand cups my pussy, his thumb lazily rubbing over my clit through my panties.

"Both," I whimper.

"Are you sure? Because once I'm inside of you, you're mine, Harlow. There will be no turning back. I'll make sure that one time with me will never be enough."

No, I'm not sure. But that doesn't seem to matter one fucking iota.

I undo his belt, then his slacks. Reaching my hand into his

boxer briefs, I wrap my fingers around his hard, thick length and pump once.

"Fuck me… Malachi."

With lightning-fast movements, Malachi divests himself of his clothes, and then removes the rest of mine. He lifts me up and presses me into the wall with his body. I wrap my legs around his hips, moaning at the friction of his dick on my clit.

"I told you before that I'd introduce you to heaven," he growls. "Brace yourself."

That's all the warning I get before he lines himself up to my center and thrusts forward, burying himself in my heat. He fills me completely, in more ways than one, in ways I don't want to acknowledge.

Malachi's strokes are long, fevered, desperate. When he dips his head and sucks a nipple into his mouth, all sensations converge, mix and swirl to cause a brutal explosion from the inside out.

"That's it, *bella*," he says. "Come apart for me."

His hips don't let up as he chases his own release and prolongs mine. With his tongue assaulting my nipple, and his fingers bruising the flesh on my thighs, he thrusts. Once, twice, three times…

Malachi stiffens as his cock pulses, sending liquid heat deep inside me.

He holds me in place for several long seconds, his face still resting against my chest. I let my arms fall from his shoulders to my sides, and that's when he pulls back to set me on my feet and looks into my eyes.

I open and close my mouth several times, trying to say something, anything, to break the sudden tension in the room. But what is there to say?

I'm sorry? No, because I'm not. Thanks for the fuck? No, that's not right either. How about round two? No. Well, that one does have possibilities.

No!

"Don't overthink it," Malachi says quietly as he takes a step back.

The moment he does, an unrelenting cold seeps into my bones.

What the fucking hell have I done?

CHAPTER 12

Malachi

HARLOW'S OVERTHINKING IT. With fascination, I watched her face register pure bliss, then morph, over and over, to confusion, indecision… regret. That's the one that's wreaking havoc on my own thoughts.

I should probably apologize for what just happened, but I can't. Because I'm not sorry. Not even a little bit. I thought I'd be introducing Harlow to heaven, but the woman turned the tables and dragged me along with her.

"That wasn't my intention when I kissed you," I finally say, needing to fill the silence.

It's true. After seeing Harlow go from badass biker bitch, ready to defend what's hers, to soft and sweet with that little girl who hugged her, I had to kiss her. Had to taste her, regardless of the consequences. She's a dichotomy of good and bad, soft and hard, sugar and spice. The more I'm around her, the more I want to explore both sides.

But I never intended to fuck her. That was just a pleasant, unexpected bonus.

Harlow bends down to pick up her clothes and starts dressing. I silently mourn the loss of her naked before me.

"Then why'd you do it?"

"Do what?"

She rolls her eyes. "Kiss me. Why'd you do that?"

I don't know how to explain it to her, the overwhelming pull she has on me, so I say it as simply as I can.

"I had to."

Harlow slips her cut back into place and shifts her gaze to mine. "You had to?"

"Yes."

"But why?"

She puts up a hard front, but right now, she can't hide her vulnerability. Don't get me wrong, her shoulders are squared, her head is held high, and her eyes are hard. But I see past that to the little things. I see the way the corners of her lips dip down slightly, hear the exasperation and uncertainty in her tone.

"Does it matter?"

"Of course it matters," she snaps, some of the vulnerability slipping away. "I wouldn't ask if it didn't."

"Why did you want to fuck me?" I counter.

Every muscle in her body tenses. The creases at the corners of her eyes deepen as she glares at me. The last vestiges of anything soft in Harlow Monroe disappear before my very eyes.

Until she takes a deep breath, holds it for several seconds, and then exhales loudly.

Harlow shrugs. "I had to."

Satisfied that I've made my point, whatever the fuck it is, I decide now is the time to shift the conversation to other matters. I'll come back to this later.

While Harlow moves to sit behind her desk, successfully putting as much distance between us as her office will allow, I get dressed. Rather than put my suit jacket on, I drape it over the back of a chair and sit across from her.

"Here." I hand her the manilla envelope that had been

tossed to the floor with my clothes. "This is everything you need to not only start, but also win a war with my family."

Harlow hesitates for a moment before snatching the envelope from my hand. But she doesn't open it. No, she simply sets it on her desk and leans back in her chair.

"Let's assume for a second that I actually believe you're giving me accurate information," she begins. "Why? What could you possibly hope to gain from this?"

"I have my reasons."

"Not good enough, Ricci."

A growl erupts from my throat at her return to using my last name, even though I understand it. We're enemies right now. Whatever we were five minutes ago might as well not have been. I get it, but I don't have to like it.

"Let's just say this is me being a loyal and decent human being."

"Bullshit."

"Maybe, maybe not. But it's all you're getting."

Harlow looks like she wants to argue, like there are words sitting on the tip of her tongue, lunging toward the freedom spewing them would provide. She says nothing though as she sits forward and opens the envelope.

She pulls page after page of documents out, scanning them as she does. At times, her eyes widen, and at others, they narrow. I know what she's seeing, what she's reading. Her reactions come as no surprise.

After she gets through the last piece of paper, she raises her head and pins me with a pain-filled stare. "The treaty never meant anything to your family, did it? It was never going to be followed. It was a means to an end."

I want to reach across her desk and cup her cheek, offer her comfort I have no right to offer. I know what that treaty cost her. I know how drastically her life changed the night it was signed. I *know,* and it's just one of the many reasons I put my plan into motion. One of the wrongs that fuel my need to make things right.

I don't reach out though. Because we're enemies. Because I know my touch would burn her right now as sure as if I lit a match and set it to her skin. But I do give her the only thing I can.

"For what it's worth, she didn't suffer."

I don't know if that's true or not, I wasn't there. But truth or lie, it's what I have. Sometimes the kindest thing a person can do, the *decent* thing a person can do, is tell someone what they need to hear, regardless of the facts.

This is one of those times.

Despair flashes in Harlow's emerald irises, and her hand flies to her mouth to stifle the cry I can hear bubbling in her throat. My heart cracks at the devastation she's trying to keep at bay. I look away, giving her as much privacy as the situation allows to collect herself.

It takes a few minutes, but eventually, the sound of her clearing her throat pulls my attention from the random pictures on the wall, the ones full of family, of life, of happiness. My family killed that. Or a part of it anyway.

Harlow stands up and gathers the contents of the envelope in her hands, pretending as if I didn't just open up Pandora's box with three words that, in and of themselves, are harmless. And I pretend that I don't see the glassy sheen in her eyes or the way her throat continues to work as she swallows her pain.

"I've got church," she says as she walks around her desk to the door. "Wait here."

The snick of the lock engaging might as well have been a bomb, it's so loud in the now empty space.

Locked in again.

CHAPTER 13

Harlow

LEANING my back against my office door, I try to suck in a breath, but the air is thick, too thick to enter my lungs.

She didn't suffer.

Inside that office, with Malachi so near, I was able to hold myself together, keep the very thin thread of composure intact. But out here in the hallway, away from him and alone, it snaps.

She didn't suffer.

I stumble down the hallway toward church, tears streaming down my face, blindly grabbing at the wall for support with one hand and clutching papers in the other.

She didn't suffer.

"Har?"

Tahiti's voice cuts through the onslaught of emotions, and I force my feet to stop moving. Her arms come around my shoulders to help me stand.

"What's wrong?" She darts her eyes around us. "Where is he? What did he do?"

I shake my head, speaking impossible.

"Har, you need to talk to me. What the fuck happened?"

She didn't suffer.

"He…" I swallow. "How, um…" I try to suck in air again, and thankfully, I get two lungs full. I breathe in, out, in, out. Then I turn what I know are bloodshot eyes to Tahiti. "How did she die? How did they kill her?"

Tahiti blanches at the question. We've never talked about the specifics of her death. The recount of events never gets that far. The conversation always ends the same, with whoever is talking reminding me of how much my mother loved me, how she did what she did for me and so many others. But the actual mechanics of how Antonio Ricci stole Lillith Monroe's last breath has never been said out loud, at least not to me.

"Tell me," I snarl when Tahiti remains quiet. "I need to know."

She didn't suffer.

Silence.

"Tell me right the fuck now, T. Or get out." I don't mean it. I'd never kick her out of the club. But I want her to understand how badly I need her to answer me. "Tell. Me!" I shout.

"A single bullet between the eyes."

An all-consuming misery grips my soul and rips it from my body in the form of a strangled cry. I collapse to the floor, my legs no longer able to support my weight. The grief is too heavy, the heartbreak too much.

She didn't suffer.

Malachi told me the truth… to a degree. My mother didn't physically suffer. Her death was quick, likely painless. But she suffered, fuck did she suffer. Because she saw it coming. She knew exactly what was happening, was aware of the moment the trigger was pulled, even if for a fraction of a second. And the last thing she saw before she died were the eyes of pure evil.

She didn't suffer.

She motherfucking suffered in all the ways that matter.

Tahiti slides down the wall and pulls me into her arms.

She rocks me, much like she would when I was little and Mom would ask her to tuck me in at night if she couldn't. She murmurs against my hair. What, I don't know, but it doesn't matter. I soak up every single slice of comfort she's giving me.

Sounds drift in and out of my awareness. Doors opening and closing, rushed footsteps, and hushed voices. I tune it all out for what feels like hours but is really only minutes. Eventually, I cry myself out.

"Thank you," I say weakly.

"Don't know what the fuck you're thanking me for, Har," Tahiti bites out.

"For telling me." I sit up and scrub my hands over my face. "I needed to know."

"No, you didn't," she insists. "But you're welcome."

I scoot to sit against the wall and rest my forearms on my knees. "You know I'd never kick you out of the club, right? Not for that anyway."

"I know." Tahiti chuckles. "But if I break any of the bylaws, betray the club or some shit, I better watch out, huh?"

"Exactly."

"Understood."

Tahiti stands and stretches an arm out to help me up. We walk the rest of the way down the hall to church, but before I can open the door, her hand on my shoulder stops me.

"I'm not gonna have to go drag your ass off the beach in the morning, am I?" she asks, referring to how she found me the other day after my tequila binge.

I shake my head.

"Good."

Five minutes later, DHMC officers file into the room. Peppermint stares at my face a little too long, concern etched in the lines on her forehead, but she says nothing. I'm grateful for her discretion and have no doubt I'll pay for it later.

"Where's the Italian prince?" Spooks asks as she takes her

seat. "You didn't kill him yet, did you? Because I was really hoping to take part in that."

"He's alive. And locked in my office."

"And you're not worried about him being in there alone?" Mama asks.

Honestly, I hadn't even considered it when I locked him in there. I had other things on my mind. But I can't tell them that.

"Nah. Everything important is in the safe. He'll be fine."

"Let's get started," Peppermint says. "It's late, we're all tired, and this might be the last chance we get to have a decent night's sleep anytime soon."

"She's right," I agree and dive right in. "Because, according to Malachi, in less than forty-eight hours, we'll officially be at war with the Italians."

"And you believe him, Prez?" This from Giggles.

"I don't think we have the luxury of not believing him." I slide the papers Malachi gave me across the table to Story. "I need you to check into all of this, see if you can verify it all, make sense of it."

"What is it?" she asks as she starts to scan the documents.

"Bank records, maps, schedules, names and addresses, blueprints, communication among the Ricci family." I shrug. "It's a lot. But if it's a lot of nothing, we need to know."

"Got it."

"I'm specifically interested in the schedules, bank records, and communications. We know that they're involved in sex trafficking, but I want to know who all is involved." What I don't say is I need to know if Malachi is involved and just playing me or if he can be trusted. "I wanna know how they do it, where they do it, their exchange points, everything. If they get a five-minute break every day to take a shit, I want to know."

"And what is all of this going to tell us?" Spooks asks. She has an ax in her hand and she's running her fingertip along the edge of the blade.

"It'll give us insight into when and where they're most vulnerable. Every piece of information can be used to inform our decisions, to mold our plan so that we're as successful as humanly possible in taking them down."

"And if it's all bogus?"

"Then I'll cut Malachi's throat myself before hunting the rest of the Ricci Crime Family down and ending their miserable lives. And I won't stop until they're all dead, or I am."

"Prez, I hate to throw a wrench into things," Peppermint begins. "But we supposedly have less than forty-eight hours. Is that enough time to sort through all this, make a plan, and then execute said plan before the Italians can make their move?"

"It'll have to be."

CHAPTER 14

Malachi

WAITING.

It seems I'm destined to always be kept waiting by Harlow. Fortunately, I have a call to make that can fill some of my time.

I tap the call button on my cell screen and listen to the ring, one time, two times, three, four, five.

"Hello."

"Things have changed," I tell him, not bothering with pleasantries.

"What the fuck, Malachi?" he barks. "We had the bitch where we wanted her. What happened?"

I grit my teeth at the word 'bitch'. "Her name is Harlow."

"Whatever. What happened?"

"I had to give her everything we had," I confess, wincing at how this probably sounds to him. He's been betrayed enough and the last thing I want him to think is I'm doing it too. But I'm not. I'd never betray him.

"Why? What was wrong with the plan we had?"

"My father, that's what. One of his minions heard me give Harlow more time to consider my offer. He doesn't believe for a second that I'm only doing this to grow the casino and escort business. He's suspicious, and when he's suspicious, he gets jumpy. He's ordered the war to start in two days."

"Jesus." A rustling sound filters through the line and then the clicking of a keyboard. "There's a flight to New Jersey tomorrow. I'll be on it."

"No," I say harshly. "You can't come here, and you know it. If I'm taken out in this thing, I need you to be able to take my place. You're the only one I trust to turn things around, make our name mean something other than crime, fear, and death. You stay put."

He sighs, the weight of the world seemingly in that long gush of air. "You can't take them all on yourself."

"Which is why I gave Harlow everything." I pinch the bridge of my nose. "I have to convince her to take out my father, Angelo and Nicholi, anyone associated with the trafficking. If she does that, there will be no war. The treaty will remain because I'll ensure it does. And you and I can run things the way we see fit."

"And what if the Devil's Handmaidens decide it's not their problem?"

"Listen to me, we picked them for a reason, remember? Not only is there a mutual history of hate but taking out sex traffickers is kinda their thing. She'll agree. They all will. Because they won't be able to live with themselves if they don't. Not with the information I've given them."

"I hope you're right." He pauses. "Have you talked to your father more since a few days ago?"

"No. He sent Nicholi to my house though. I'll go see him tomorrow, show my face and convince him I'm on the right side. I'll play my part, like I always do."

"I know you will, Malachi. I'm not worried about that."

"Then what are you worried about?"

"He's your father, Malachi. He's dying. That's gotta resonate with you on some level, regardless of how much you hate him."

There was a time he'd be right, but that time is long past. Besides, I'm not alone in this department. My father isn't the only parent who won't survive this. I'm not the only son losing their sperm donor.

"How are you doing with it?" I ask.

"My father disowned me a long time ago. He's already dead to me."

"Good riddance to both of them then."

"Well, I'm here if you wanna talk about it."

"Thanks. And same goes."

"So, Harlow is it? When did she go from biker bitch to Harlow?"

I bristle at the question, although I shouldn't. He's my best friend, and I've always told him everything.

"Yes, it's Harlow. And we're gonna leave it at that, yeah?"

"Whatever you say."

"I'm hanging up now," I say, finally letting some humor seep into my tone.

I disconnect the call, but stare at my screen for a minute. Fuck, I miss him.

Before I can slide my phone into my pocket, it vibrates with an incoming text.

Father: Where are you?

Seriously? Last time I checked, I was a thirty-year-old man who didn't have to tell Daddy my every move. But I respond because heaven forbid I don't.

Me: At home.

Father: No, you're not. Nicholi just drove by and said your car is gone.

I roll my neck from side to side to relieve the tension this man causes me.

Me: Do you need me for something?

Father: Yes. Be at my house at 8am sharp.

Me: And you sent Nicholi to my house to tell me that?

Father: Be there. 8am. Sharp!

I guess that's my answer.

With my phone secured in my pocket, I rise from my chair and move to stand in front of the pictures on the wall, the ones I noticed earlier. Some were taken here, at their club-house, while others are outdoor snapshots, and others are photos that seem more organized.

My gaze lands on one picture in particular. It's in the middle of a framed collage and captures a moment between who I can only assume is Harlow and her mother. Harlow's features are the same, if not years younger and much more innocent, in the photo. Her hair is the same color, although she wore it a lot longer when she was little. Her mom is standing behind her, with her arms draped over Harlow's shoulders. And her chin is propped on her daughter's head.

Both of them seem to be frozen in time, captured in the split second that this image was taken. They're laughing, or based on their smiles and crinkled eyes, I assume they were at the time. It's not lost on me that there are equal parts simplicity and profoundness in the moment.

I don't have pictures like this at my house. No family photos, tiny spans of time suspended for posterity, nothing. That's not how my family worked. My mother left shortly after my brother was born, and my father removed any trace of her from my childhood home. And when Mortichi died, he disappeared from our family tree as well.

There were no happy moments, family barbecues or vacations. It was all work, all the time, and the only way I knew how to live, the only way I wanted to live. Until it wasn't.

I spin around at the sound of the door lock disengaging and watch Harlow walk in. She looks tired. Beautiful, but tired. Her eyes are rimmed in red from all the sobbing I heard her doing in the hallway and her hair is disheveled, like she's been running her hands through her short locks.

I can't stop staring, memorizing her every nuance, every feature... her.

I blink several times to refocus. "So? What's the plan?" I ask.

Before she can answer, Peppermint strides through the door, freezing when she sees me.

"Fuck, I forgot you were here."

"Nice to see you again too," I say, only looking at her out of the corner of my eye. I remain facing Harlow.

"Don't you have somewhere to be? A fancy party to attend or something?" Peppermint practically snarls the question, but her gaze bounces between me and her president.

"No, he doesn't," Harlow says before I can even open my mouth to respond. She never breaks eye contact. "He's staying here."

"Excuse me?" I snap, sure I misunderstood her.

"We're under partial lockdown," Harlow says as if that explains it all. "And in..." She lifts her stare to the clock on the wall. "... seven hours and forty-two minutes, we'll be under total lockdown."

"I don't give a shit. I can't stay here. I have a business to run, things to—"

"Listen up, Ricci," Harlow barks and I press my lips together. "You came to me. Several times now, I might add." She advances a step. "You need me, my club, what we offer."

Another step. "I don't trust you as far as I can throw you, but the fact is, I need you too." Two more steps. "If you're setting us up, then at least you'll be here and not out there plotting against us. But if you're telling me the truth, I need you here so you can give us more intel."

I should argue, keep advocating for myself and getting the hell out of here. But my brain stuttered when she said she needed me and that's all I can focus on. Harlow Monroe needs me. Granted, not in the way I want her to need me, but the fact remains… She said she needs me.

"I'm supposed to meet with my father in the morning," I tell her, not commenting on the rest of her words.

"Fuck your father," Peppermint grits out.

Shit, I forgot she was here. I finally turn to face her. "I'm trying to," I remind her. "Why do you think I'm doing all of this? Why do you think I'm here, giving you what you need to take him out? I hate my father," I seethe. "More than you can possibly imagine. But I need to meet with him in the morning or he'll know something's up. He's already suspicious."

Peppermint looks at Harlow. "Prez, you can't seriously be considering this."

Harlow takes a deep breath and closes her eyes. I wish I knew what was going on in her head, but I suspect not many people get the privilege of being that close to her. When she lifts her lids, her gaze is swimming with conviction.

"I'll get you to your meeting in the morning." Peppermint opens her mouth to speak, and Harlow shifts her attention to her. "Pep, wait in the hall for me."

"But—"

"Pep."

Peppermint grumbles, but leaves the room, the door slamming behind her.

When we're alone, Harlow closes the rest of the distance between us and tips her head to look up at me.

"I'm going to tell you the same thing I told my club." There's steel in her tone, more than I've ever heard from her. "If you're fucking with me, I'll slit your throat myself."

I bristle at the threat, annoyance clawing at me that she has absolutely zero trust in me.

Why should she trust you? You've given her no reason to.

"I'm not fucking with you."

She gives a curt nod, but if her emerald eyes could speak, they'd be saying 'not buying what you're selling'.

"Then this is how it's going to work. You may have orchestrated this whole scheme, but I'm carrying it out, I'm finishing it. This is the Devil's Handmaidens show now, and I fucking run it. You'll do what I say, when I say, no questions asked. And if I say you stay here, you stay the fuck here. My rules, always."

This is what some would call a crossroads. A choice has to be made whether to turn left or right. If I choose left, I can remain the man I was trained to be: a leader, heir to a throne, ruthless. I can be feared, revered, respected. Malachi Ricci, son of Antonio Ricci, future king of the Atlantic City criminal underworld. My legacy will be won on the backs of others and bathed in their blood.

Or I can choose to go right and become the man I want to be: Malachi Ricci, don of the Ricci Crime Family. I'll still be respected, but more than that, I'll be trusted. I'll be ruthless when I need to be but fair at all times. I can rule the criminal underworld in my city the way I want to, without humans being the product we deal in. I can be a villain to many, but a good man to those who matter. My legacy will mean something, and it will be earned.

Either way, I win. My father will die, as will his biggest supporters and anyone involved in the trafficking I despise so much. But only one direction will allow me to look at myself in the mirror each day and not hate what I see.

And only one requires me to do what I've always done

and am desperately trying to never have to do again: follow. I'm a born leader, but that's been damped my entire life by my father. Harlow's doing the same, but I find with her, I don't mind so much. In fact, I'm okay with it if it means I can become the man I want to be and not the man I was trained to be.

"Done."

Harlow's eyes widen. "Seriously? You're fine to sit back and let me take it from here?"

I understand her reluctance to believe me. And maybe she should be, because I'm not going to completely roll over. I want to be a part of this till the end. I want to be there when my father, Angelo, and Nicholi take their last breaths.

Taking a chance, I lift my hand to her face and cup her cheek. "I'll never just sit back. I don't have it in me to do that." I glide my thumb under her eye and savor the way she leans into my caress. "But as long as you don't completely cut me out of the carnage, I'll follow your lead. But you have to understand something."

"What's that?"

"I have to be able to keep up appearances. My family can't know that I'm with you on this. Not until I want them to know. That means I can't hide out here. I'll stay here at night if you insist." Honestly, I can't think of a better place to spend my nights if it means I'll be close to her. I don't say that though. "But I need to be visible during the day."

Harlow straightens away from me, and I let my arm fall.

"Fine. But you and I?" She flicks her hand between our bodies. "We're joined at the hip. I still don't trust you, which means I go where you go. And you only go if I approve it."

"Done."

"Just like that?"

"Just like that."

"You'll follow my orders, no questions asked?"

"I can't promise no questions, *bella*," I tell her honestly.

"But I'll follow orders. If that's what it takes to prove to you that I'm on your side, I'll set aside my ego and follow instead of lead."

Harlow narrows her eyes, almost squinting like she's trying to dissect my intentions. She must like what she sees because again, she nods. Then she turns away and walks to the door.

"Gimme a few minutes and then I'll show you to a room."

CHAPTER 15
Harlow

"WHAT THE FUCK are you doing, Har?"

I pull my office door shut behind me, not bothering to lock it this time, and take a deep breath. Peppermint is pacing the hallway, arms crossed over her chest and eyes blazing. I follow her movements for a minute while I think about how to respond.

What the fuck am I doing?

The truth is, I have no clue. I always relied on that treaty and thought we were safe from an all-out war. It's the reason my mother died, and I intended to honor that. But then Malachi walked into Devil's Double Down and fucking spun my world on its axis like a goddamn dreidle.

I know that Peppermint thinks I'm crazy for keeping Malachi here. Hell, I probably am. But I meant it when I said I don't trust him.

You trusted him enough to fuck him.

Malachi is a means to an end. He stays here and I can keep an eye on him so he can't cause us more trouble. As the saying goes, keep your friends close but your enemies closer.

"I'm trying to get us through this the best way I know

how," I finally say, averting my gaze when Peppermint halts a few feet in front of me.

She stares at me, silently, for several minutes, scrutinizing, analyzing, searching. "You like him," she accuses.

She always could read me. From the moment we met, I've never been able to hide anything from her. It's part of the reason we work so well together. Peppermint keeps me honest.

But I don't want to be honest about this.

"Of course I don't like him," I protest, but I can hear the lie in my tone. And if I can hear it, so can she.

"Admit it, Har." She takes a step toward me, and I take a step back. Her brow arches at the action. She takes another step, as do I. Her face falls. "Fucking hell," she mutters.

"What?"

"I thought I sensed something between the two of you in there," she says, pointing to my office door. "The way he looked at you, the way your cheeks flushed." Peppermint throws her hands up. "And the smell. Jesus, Har, I could smell the sex. But I told myself I was crazy, imagining things because Harlow Monroe would never fuck the enemy. She's better than that." My best friend pauses to take a breath, her chest heaving with the intake of air. "Unless fucking Malachi is part of your plan. Did you whore yourself out to him, Har? Is that—"

The crack of my palm on Peppermint's cheek is so loud I don't hear my office door swing open. The shock on my VP's face mimics my own at having struck her and only intensifies when Malachi wraps his hand around her throat and shoves her against the wall.

"Harlow isn't a whore," he thunders. "Just because you don't understand something doesn't automatically make it wrong."

Peppermint's eyes dart from Malachi to me and back

again. I shake off my surprise at his actions and lunge forward to grab his wrist.

"Let her go," I demand.

"She insulted you."

"Not the first time and won't be the last," I tell him.

I recognize the look in Malachi's eyes, the absolute malice he wants to unleash. I have no doubt he'd kill her if I weren't standing here, but he's not. No, he couldn't have done that already. He's holding back for a reason.

I tug on his arm, but he doesn't budge, so I dig my nails into his skin, hard enough to draw blood. I'll use my hatchet if I have to, but I'm hoping it doesn't come to that. Because Peppermint was right. I like him.

"Let. Her. Go."

Malachi shifts his gaze to me and blinks several times. Then he drops his arm and Peppermint doubles over, gasping for breath. I reach for her to make sure she's okay, but she shakes off my attempt and storms down the hall.

I whirl on Malachi. "What the fuck was that?"

"I didn't appreciate the way she was talking to you."

"Too damn bad," I snap.

"If you think I'm going to sit back and listen—"

I stab a finger at his chest, backing him up with each step forward I take. "That's exactly what I think. My rules, remember?" Malachi runs into the wall. "I'm not some damsel in distress who needs you or any man to come save me. In case you haven't noticed, none of the women in this club are your average female. We're going to fight, we're going to say hurtful things. But we'll get over it. And we'll do all of that without a man at our sides."

A thoughtful expression crosses his features, like he's seeing me, *really* seeing me for the first time. "I'm sorry."

I sigh. "I'm not the one you need to apologize to." I glance over my shoulder in the direction Peppermint went and then return my attention back to the brute who will be my shadow for fuck knows how long. "Put your hands on one of my girls again and you'll regret it."

Malachi lifts his lips into a grin. "The whole 'I'll slit your throat' thing?"

My lips twitch at his retort. Fucker has a sense of humor, I'll give him that. "Something like that."

"Understood." He dips his gaze, and his nostrils flare. "What will happen if I put my hands on you?" His tone is gruff, gravely as if it pains him to be this close and not touch me.

I'll come apart, splinter into a million ecstasy filled pieces.

"I don't know."

"Hmm." Malachi clears his throat and then his eyes travel in the direction Peppermint went. "Should you go talk to her or something? I can, uh, apologize now."

Flustered by the rapid switch in topic, I take a deep breath and force myself to focus on the here and now and not the fantasies assaulting my mind. "Nah. Morning is soon enough. She needs space to cool down." I smile sadly. "Like I said, not the first time and won't be the last."

Malachi shoves his hands in his pockets and rocks back on his heels. "So, my room?"

"Right." I turn and start down the hall. "Follow me."

I don't have a spare room for him, so he's going to be bunking with me. Rather than tell him, I simply walk through the clubhouse, not bothering to stop in the main room and talk to anyone, and up the stairs to my suite. I have a condo in the city, but I'm rarely there, so I made sure I had enough space for everything I need here too.

All of the club officers have their own bedrooms, with attached baths. There's also a large bunk room for prospects, a weapon's room, small gym, and two bathrooms on the main floor. In the basement is where we keep a holding cell, in case we need it.

I pull my keys out of my cut when we reach my door and

unlock it. Then I step aside and extend my arm to let him enter first. As soon as he crosses the threshold, he turns and extends his arm above his head to lean on the door frame.

Oh, this should be interesting. He thinks he's staying in here alone. I can work with this.

"What time do you need to meet with your father?" I ask.

"Eight. Which means if I actually show up at eight, I'm late. I need to leave by seven fifteen."

"We."

"Huh?"

"*We* need to leave by seven fifteen. Joined at the hip, remember?"

"Right. And what will you be doing while I'm inside his house? Because I can assure you, if you try to go inside, it won't end well for you."

I arch a brow. "Is that a threat?"

"No, Harlow. It's a promise. My father will not allow you to step foot into his home."

I wave my hand like it's no big deal.

"I'll handle it. I've got a plan."

"Care to fill me in?"

"No."

Malachi rolls his eyes, clearly exasperated with me. "I suppose this is what you meant by me following orders, no questions asked."

"Now you're starting to understand."

"Fine." Malachi leans forward and looks down the hall. "So, where's your room? Ya know, in case I need permission to take a leak in the middle of the night."

I grin and duck under his arm to stroll inside. "We're standing in it." I turn around to stare at his back.

Malachi groans before lowering his arm and his head. "Of course we are."

"Be a doll and flip the lock," I say with saccharine sweetness, just to ruffle his feathers.

"Yes, ma'am," he mumbles before shutting and locking the door.

I move to my dresser and dig through my clothes to find something that might fit for him to sleep in. My hand lands on a pair of black sweats that were Jack's. They're about the same height, although Malachi is more powerfully built than Jack is, so they may be a bit tight.

My tongue darts out to swipe over my bottom lip as I picture Malachi with his junk bulging behind the cotton material. Fuck, this is probably a very bad idea.

That thought is only compounded when strong hands settle on my hips and Malachi presses his front to my back. For a moment, I forget that this is a bad idea and push my ass back, reveling in the groan that he releases near my ear.

Malachi's right hand slips beneath my tee and flattens on my stomach. Heat spreads through my veins, and my pussy throbs. But this isn't happening. Not right now.

I shove his hands away from me and spin to slap the pants into his chest.

"Here, these should work."

Again, I duck under his arm and go into the bathroom to change myself. After brushing my teeth and giving myself a pep talk on not sleeping with the enemy, again, I reenter the bedroom and freeze.

Malachi is stretched out on the bed, completely naked. The black sweats I gave him are draped over the end of the mattress and he's grinning like the damn cat that ate the canary. And let's not forget his thick cock, which is standing at attention.

"What the hell are you doing?" I snarl.

"Going to bed."

"Nope." I point to the pants. "Put those on." He doesn't move. "Don't make me get my hatchet," I threaten. Still, he doesn't budge. I heave a sigh. "Please."

Malachi's grin softens as he sits up. "Since you asked so nicely."

Once he has the sweats on, I see that I was right. They're too tight.

Fuck. Me.

"You can sleep on the couch."

Malachi glances at the loveseat along the opposite wall as my bed then back to me. "I'd rather sleep in the bed. Bad back."

Bullshit.

"Couch!" I shout, my anger spiking, both at him and myself for allowing him to get to me.

Malachi must sense my frustration because he stands.

'Yes, ma'am."

CHAPTER 16
Malachi

"HOW CAN you be so sure this will work?"

Harlow's been staring out the passenger window since we left the clubhouse ten minutes ago, but she looks my direction at my question.

"I'm not," she admits. "But it's worth a shot."

I don't understand her logic. After she got a shower this morning, I started to grill her about her plan. She didn't want to give me any details at first, but once I explained that I can only play my part correctly if I know what's going on, she caved.

Her brilliant idea is to throw herself at my father's mercy and ask *him* for more time to consider the offer I made to purchase Devil's Double Down. Her logic is that by going to him, she's showing him respect. She also reminded me that, as far as my father is concerned, she knows nothing about a war.

Her logic is flawed, completely fucking fucked. But as she also politely reminded me, with her hatchet pointing to my crotch, her game, her rules.

So here I am, trying not to sweat a river under my Armani suit while navigating morning traffic, and mentally calculating all the potential ways I might have to kill someone today if they try to hurt her.

Fun times.

I grip the steering wheel, and my knuckles turn white under the pressure.

"You don't know my father, Harlow. This is a suicide mission."

"And I told you, I can take care of myself. The question is, can you take care of yourself, if it comes to that?"

"I can get out of there if I have to. But the repercussions won't be pretty."

She shrugs. "Who cares?"

"I care," I snap.

"Why? You said you had your reasons for doing this, so unless you were blowing smoke up my ass, think about those."

"Which is exactly why I care."

"And exactly why you shouldn't. No matter how this plays out, Malachi, you've gone against your family. There's no coming back from that. You set this plan in motion, now grow a pair and see it through."

I spare her a glare, narrowing my eyes. Harlow only continues on.

"This is going to end one of two ways. Either you're going to get what you want, whatever that is beyond the death of your father, uncle, and cousin. Or you're going to die. Is your endgame worth dying for?"

An image of Mina flashes in my mind, and I hear her begging me to run away with her. It morphs to her lying in a pool of blood, a bullet hole in her head, with my father standing over her, gun still raised. I think about her, about all of them. All of the trafficking victims my family has left in its wake.

I think about my best friend, ostracized from his family. I remember the way he was discarded like some broken toy because he didn't fall in line. I think about all the good he and I can do if he could only come home.

I think about Mortichi, my brother, about how he died because he was groomed to be as vile as the rest of the Ricci's. He was only seventeen and didn't stand a chance because of my father.

And I think about Harlow, about how she's surprised me at every turn. About how she's sitting next to me, ready to run straight toward the fire, even though she has no clue just how hot it can burn. She doesn't even completely trust me, yet here she is.

Am I prepared to die for my endgame? Am I prepared to risk my life in the name of vengeance? Am I willing to sacrifice myself, should it come to that, so that so many others might have a chance to live their lives without the threat of my father hanging over their heads?

The simple answer is yes. It's all worth dying for.

The much more complicated answer, the unvarnished, truthful answer is it's worth it, but I'm not ready to die.

I'm so close to eliminating those who stand for all the wrong things, to rising up and taking over. I want to see that through. I want to be here, alive and breathing, to live my dream of a life out from under my father's rule.

And I really want to explore whatever the hell is between me and the woman next to me. Because something tells me it could be good. Really fucking good.

"Well?" Harlow prods when I don't respond. "Is it worth dying for?"

"Yes."

"Then let those balls drop." She punches me in the arm. "We've got work to do."

———

"I don't recall giving you permission to show up with a woman in tow."

I'm standing in my father's office, my back to the door. My father is sitting in his chair, Uncle Angelo and Nicholi flanking him on either side. I feel like I'm in front of a firing squad, but I don't let it show.

When Harlow and I were greeted at the door, we were immediately led to the parlor and instructed to wait. One would think I'd be allowed to go where I want in the home I grew up in, but no. I haven't been able to do that since I was eighteen and moved out on my own.

Thirty minutes passed before I was summoned. Now that I'm standing here, I know why we had to wait. My father saw Harlow on the security cameras and decided to be moved from his bed to his office. It's a power play, plain and simple.

"You didn't say to come alone either," I counter.

"Watch your tone with me, Malachi," my father clips out, his tone deceptively strong. "I'm still in charge."

"Yes, sir." It takes every ounce of restraint to not tack on a snide 'for now', but I manage.

Uncle Angelo steps around the desk and comes to stand directly in front of me. "You should know, your father and I are divided on his decision to bring you here today. Quite frankly, the only reason I finally gave in is because my idiot son opened his mouth and told you about our plans to start a war with the Devil's Handmaidens MC."

I spare a glance at Nicholi and see his ears redden.

"And here I thought he was sent to tell me." I clasp my hands in front of me. "Ya know, since I'm the heir and should be involved in these kinds of decisions."

"You might be your father's heir, but you're not the first in line to take over once he's gone."

"Your point?" I quirk a brow.

I know I'm pushing my uncle's buttons, probably harder than I should. But he's pissing me off.

"Enough!" My father barks. "Angelo, stand down." Uncle Angelo glares at me a moment before stepping back and returning to my father's side. "Malachi, it's no secret that I disagree with your decision to make an offer for that casino. It's foolish and brings unwanted attention from that biker club."

"I stand by my actions. If you would only hear—"

"I wasn't finished," he clips. I nod. "As I was saying, it's foolish. But the more I've had a chance to think about it, the more I think I understand."

What?

"You do?"

"I do. Granted, it's a lot of money to spend, but the income a second casino would provide will far outweigh anything we shell out. It's a solid business decision."

"I agree."

"It also opens up the door for us to wipe out the bikers once and for all. You broke the treaty by going into Devil's Double Down so I'm sure there will be consequences. Although I'm surprised none have come our way yet." He waves a frail hand. "But that's beside the point. The treaty is broken. Now, it's no surprise that I didn't much care to abide by the treaty. Trafficking is too lucrative for that. But it did give the bikers a false sense of security, allowing us to operate under their noses without fear of retaliation."

"And an endless supply of grade A—"

"Shut up, Nicholi!" Uncle Angelo seethes.

"It's okay, Angelo," my father assures him. "The boy is right. We have enjoyed our share of the product."

Mina flashes through my mind, and my clasped hands ache from how hard I'm squeezing to keep myself from lashing out.

"Anyway, you broke the treaty, and I'm left to clean up your mess. While I don't condone Nicholi running his mouth to you, it's good you know about the impending war. It will give you the opportunity to prove your loyalty to this family once and for all."

"You question my loyalty?" I ask.

He should, but it irritates me that he actually does.

"I've questioned your loyalty since Mina's tragic and untimely death. You've been… *different* since then."

He means I haven't been the same monster he raised me to be.

"Just because I don't take part in the trafficking side of things anymore doesn't mean I'm disloyal." I force myself to relax, to let my arms fall to my sides. "I've had a casino to run, an empire to build, one in which you put me in charge of. Or have you forgotten that? Have the millions of dollars I've made for this family meant nothing?"

"Money isn't everything, Malachi. It's a means to an end, that is all. Power. That's what matters. Power and the Ricci name, both of which are synonymous with the product we procure and supply." My father pauses, takes a shaky breath. "And loyalty. You and Nicholi are the only two left in your generation. With Mortichi buried in the ground and Nico… Well, that's another matter. Nicholi has proved himself time and time again. He spills blood in the name of loyalty. Can you say the same?"

It's a rhetorical question, so I say nothing.

"I guess we shall see."

My father presses the intercom button on his desk.

"Please escort Miss Monroe to my office."

CHAPTER 17
Harlow

"MR. RICCI WILL SEE YOU NOW."

I move away from the window and follow the butler—seriously? A damn butler?—down a series of hallways. I log every turn, every doorway, every possible escape route as we walk. This place is massive, bigger than I could have imagined, despite having seen the blueprints. I studied those last night when I couldn't sleep. They'd been a part of what Malachi had provided in that damn manilla envelope, and I'm glad he did.

A smile creeps over my face as I recall Malachi's annoyance when we pulled into the driveway.

"This is a joke, right?" I ask, staring out the window at the ginormous mansion.

"What?"

"You grew up here?"

"Unfortunately."

I shift my stare from the structure to the man in the driver's seat. "Malachi, this isn't a house, it's a fucking castle."

"You don't think I know that?"

"Sorry," I say, sensing I touched a nerve.

"Let's just get this over with."

Malachi bursts from the car and comes around to open my door. And to my consternation, I sit there and wait for him to do so.

"This isn't at all what I pictured," I tell him.

"It's not?"

I shake my head. "I know you come from money, and I know your family is a big deal. I mean, who doesn't? But this is ridiculous."

Malachi chuckles. "Thanks. I think."

When the butler stops in front of a set of double doors, I gawk at the ornateness of them. The wood is a dark cherry, and they arch at the top. There are intricate carvings of symbols of some sort. And then there's the knobs. The ugly gold knobs that are no doubt real.

Fugly!

The butler is simply standing there like a statue, and I don't know if I'm supposed to wait for the doors to be opened or what, so I decide to grab the bull by the horns, so to speak, and do what I'd do in any other situation. I grip the knobs, shove those babies open myself, and stride right the fuck into Antonio Ricci's outrageously ugly office.

"Hi boys."

Malachi groans.

The two men standing on either side of who I assume is Antonio glare. And Antonio, the arrogant, sickly-looking bastard, smiles.

"Please, come in, Miss Monroe." He waves his hand to a chair situated across from him. "Have a seat."

"I think I'll stand, thanks."

I swivel my head from side to side as if I'm taking in the decor when in actuality, I'm scanning for weapons. Or anything that could be used as one. My hand moves to the hatchet sheathed at my waist of its own volition.

Antonio watches me intently, and his eyes narrow when he sees my movement. "There's no need for that here, Miss Monroe. We have a treaty, after all."

Breathe, Har. In, out, in, out. Don't kill him. Not yet.

I force my arm to relax. "You're right, of course." I shrug. "Some habits are hard to break."

"I understand," Antonio says. "Now, my son informs me that you wish to speak with me. Is this true?"

Duh, asshole. I'm here, aren't I?

I look at Malachi, but he simply stares straight ahead. If I didn't know any better, I'd think he was catatonic and not even aware I'm in the room.

Good. He's playing his part.

He better be fucking playing.

"Yes, sir." I take a deep breath and continue. "I wanted to speak to you about his offer to purchase my casino."

"I'm listening."

I take a deep breath and brace myself for what I'm about to say. *You've got this, Har. Just hang in there a little longer.*

"I accept."

"What?" Malachi barks, snapping out of his stupor and whipping his head in my direction.

Don't fuck this up, man. Please don't fuck this up.

"Son, is there a problem?" Antonio asks, watching his son closely.

Malachi's eyes narrow on mine, but he quickly schools his expression and turns to his father.

"No, there's no problem. This is great news."

Hold onto that thought.

"But I do have a condition," I say, not letting them get too far into a celebration.

Antonio leans forward. "And what's that?"

I close the distance between me and Antonio's desk and brace myself with my fingers curled over the edge of the wood. I lock eyes with the man who killed my mom, stare into the same soulless eyes she did before she died.

And I feel nothing.

"You look like her," Antonio says before I can give him my condition.

Physically, I don't react to his statement. But mentally, I recoil. How dare he say that? How dare he even let her become a part of his thoughts?

We stare at one another, neither willing to break eye contact. My heartbeat thumps wildly in my ears, against my ribcage. If I didn't know better, I'd think it was about to burst from my chest.

But no, it won't. I'm stronger than that. Lillith Monroe made sure of it.

Antonio breaks first.

"So, your condition, Miss Monroe?"

I lean across his desk, closer to him than I care to be.

"Devil's Double Down is yours…" *This is it, Har. Now or never.* "… If you call off the war you're prepared to start tomorrow."

———

Six hours earlier…

"Want some company?"

I look over my shoulder at Peppermint, then throw back the rest of my tequila and slam the shot glass onto the bar.

"Sure."

She slides onto the stool next to me, grabs my empty glass and pours herself a shot, which she proceeds to gulp down. She pours another, shooting it back too, then wipes the left-over liquor from the corners of her lips.

"You know I don't think you're a whore, right?" she asks quietly.

"I know." I rest my elbow on the bar to prop my head in my hand. "How's the cheek?"

Peppermint chuckles. "Fine. You slap like a bitch."

"Ha ha." I drop my eyes to her neck. "He won't put his hands on you again."

She averts her gaze and stares at the DHMC logo behind the bar. "If he does, he won't live to see another day." Peppermint sighs. "In all seriousness though, what he did… I get it."

"What do you mean?"

"He was sticking up for you, Har." She turns back to meet my eyes. "That's all I want for you, ya know? Someone who's going to match your strength. And I don't mean physically. You deserve someone who will stand up for you, who will protect you no matter what, just because he wants to. There are plenty of guys out there who will jump in to play savior because, deep down, they don't think you can take care of yourself." She shakes her head. "But Malachi? The look in his eyes when he came through that door and slammed me against the wall? That was a man defending a woman he cares about, not because she couldn't defend herself, but because he wanted to, because he would do anything to protect her."

"Oh, come on, Pep. He was acting like an overbearing caveman."

"Maybe."

"We don't even know each other. He can't like me."

Peppermint smirks. "That didn't stop you from banging him."

I huff out a breath. "Fine. We fucked. Are you happy?"

"Yep."

"Doesn't change anything. We're enemies. We hate each other."

"Do you remember what you told me back when my family refused to let me come home?" she asks.

"Before or after I came to you with my very detailed plan to kill them?"

"Be serious, Har. What did you tell me?"

"I told you that it didn't matter. That, if they wanted to

define your worth based on a set of circumstances that were out of your control, let them. Because it said more about them than it did you."

"Exactly," she confirms. "And do you remember what you said to the club the day you were patched as our president?"

"Where is this going, Pep?"

"Do you?"

"I said that my mother left a legacy, one I was expected to carry on. But I also reminded everyone that I'm not my mother and never would be. I would carry on her legacy, turn it into my own, in the best way I knew how."

"Right." Peppermint pours another shot and slides it toward me. "Isn't it possible that all of that applies to Malachi, too? That maybe we shouldn't judge him based on the circumstances of his birth, of which he had no choice? That maybe, just maybe, he's trying to carve out his own legacy, separate and very different than that of his father?"

"Jesus, you're in a philosophical mood."

"I saw his eyes, Har. You can't fake what I saw."

"How does you seeing that he might like me in his eyes turn into all of this?" I ask and then down the shot she poured.

"It just made me think is all."

"Okay, oh wise one," I tease. "And what do you suggest I do with all of this? How the hell am I supposed to know if he's an enemy or not? It's not like I can come out and ask him. If he's setting us up, he'll just keep doing it."

"Flip the script on him," she suggests as she slides off her stool. "How he reacts will tell you everything you need to know."

CHAPTER 18

Malachi

"I ACCEPT."

There's no way I heard her right.

"What?" I bark, whipping my head in Harlow's direction. This is not what we discussed.

"Son, is there a problem?" my father asks. I know he's watching me closely, gauging my every reaction.

I narrow my eyes at Harlow, silently showing her how fucking pissed I am. But then I school my features and turn to my father.

"No, there's no problem. This is great news."

This is horrible fucking news. And so far off script.

"But I do have a condition," Harlow says, breaking through the tension in the room.

"And what's that?" my father asks her coolly.

I watch in horror as Harlow marches her tight little body up to my father's desk and makes herself comfortable as she leans on it.

Jesus.

"You look like her," my father says before Harlow opens her mouth to speak.

If a grenade exploded, it wouldn't be any louder than the

deafening silence. Of all the things my father could say, of course that would be it. This whole situation is fucked nine ways to Sunday, and he just made it a million times worse.

There's no telling how Harlow will react to that comment. I brace myself for it but am surprised when she does nothing but stare. I imagine her face is a mask of rage, but maybe not. Clearly, she's a better actress than I thought she would be.

She had me fooled completely on what the plan was.

"So, your condition, Miss Monroe?" my father prods.

Harlow leans across his desk so there's barely room for any more than a feather between them.

"Devil's Double Down is yours…" *She pauses, her shoulders moving with a deep breath.* "… If you call off the war you're prepared to start tomorrow."

What the actual fuck?

With that simple statement, she's single handedly assured my death. She's unraveled the plan that has been years in the making.

She must have a reason.

Without thinking, I do the first thing that comes to mind. I lunge forward to yank Harlow's hatchet out of the sheath at her waist and slice it across my father's throat. Then I scoop her up and throw her over my shoulder. I barrel through the double doors and down the hall.

My uncle and cousin must be shocked by my action because it takes a minute for chaos to ensue. I'm down two of the hallways before I hear footsteps thundering behind us.

Gunshots ring out, and wood splinters as each bullet misses and lodges into the walls around us.

"Put me down!" Harlow shouts, pounding at my back.

"Shut up. I'll deal with you when there aren't bullets flying at my head."

"Malachi! You're a dead man!"

Uncle Angelo's voice is booming. But I tune it out and

focus on getting myself and the screaming banshee of a woman in my arms out of here alive.

"You better run far, cousin!" Nicholi shouts, his voice echoing in the cavernous hallways.

When I reach the front door, I don't slow down, but ram it with the shoulder I don't have Harlow slung over, and race down the steps toward my car. I open the back door on the driver's side and unceremoniously dump Harlow in the backseat and toss her hatchet to the floor.

I yank open my door and climb in to crank the engine. Stomping on the gas, I tear out of my father's driveway. I don't let up until we reach the highway and I'm forced to slow down due to traffic.

Harlow leans forward between the driver and passenger seats. "Well, that was fun."

Rage. Red hot rage swirls through my veins. If I were the man I was groomed to be, I'd pull over and end her life for the stunt she just pulled. But I'm not that man. And as mad as I am, I keep a tight hold on the last thought I had before slitting my father's throat: she must have a reason.

Although, I'm not interested in it right now.

When I say nothing, Harlow sits back and wisely shuts her goddamn mouth.

And I drive. I weave in and out of traffic, take random exits and roads to ensure we aren't followed, until two hours later I'm pulling up in front of the gate of the DHMC clubhouse.

All the while, I'm silent. Seething. Thinking.

"Uh, why are you in the back, Prez?" the woman at the gate asks Harlow when I roll her window down so she can get us inside.

"He's pissed at me, Vinnie," she says, with what I imagine is a very pleased with herself grin.

Pissed is an understatement.

"Ah, gotcha. And the blood on his hands? Not yours, right?" Vinnie asks.

Blood?

I lift my hands from the steering wheel and see that Vinnie is indeed correct. There's blood. Lots of blood.

"His father's," Harlow says.

"Oh shit. Well, okay then."

Two seconds later the gate slides open, and I pull up to the clubhouse. I don't make any move to get out, though, and neither does Harlow.

"We can't sit out here forever," she says. When I remain silent, I hear the back door open and then another door, just before she slides into the passenger seat. She rests her bloody hatchet on her lap. "I know this isn't your first kill, so that's not the issue here."

I slowly turn my head to face her. My mouth opens and closes several times before any words come out.

"I keep telling myself you have your reasons for doing that, for throwing me under the bus like that. I keep telling myself that you wouldn't have betrayed me like that unless there was a real fucking good reason." I tilt my head. "But I also keep reminding myself that I don't know you at all, so maybe you didn't." My eyes narrow. "Please tell me you had your reasons."

Harlow swallows. "I did."

"Care to share them?"

"No, not really."

"Are you fucking kidding me?!" I shout, punching the steering wheel and honking the horn in the process. "You just destroyed my life and you're not even going to tell me why?!"

"That's not what I said." Her voice is even, controlled.

"Quit playing games, Harlow," I growl.

Harlow sits back against the seat and stares out the front window. "Malachi, you're a smart man. If you stop for a second and use that brain of yours, it would be pretty crystal fucking clear why I did what I did."

"I'm not in the mood to think. I'm in the mood to kill. And unless you want me to act on that, I suggest you spell it out for me. Why. Did. You. Do. It?"

"To flip the script."

"Mission accomplished. But why?"

Harlow shakes her head. "It's not that easy to explain."

"Try!" I yell, my voice vibrating with fury.

For a moment, I don't think she's going to answer, but then she turns to look at me. And all of my anger starts to float away at the sight of tears in her eyes. I watch as she swallows, time and time again, trying to regain some composure. Harlow's strong, that's for sure, but she's losing the battle.

"You wouldn't understand."

Harlow grips the handle and pushes the door open before stumbling out and racing to the clubhouse door. She disappears inside before I really even register that she's running away from me.

I throw open my door and race inside after her, only to be stopped by a line of DHMC members with looks that could kill as quickly as Harlow's hatchet can.

"Where is she?" I ask, swinging my gaze from one to the next.

"What happened?" Peppermint demands as she takes a step forward.

For a second, I wonder if she's going to lash out for what happened last night, but she doesn't. She must take my hesitation to respond as me not wanting to talk to anyone else, so she turns to face the group.

"Get gone everyone. We need a minute."

The others disperse, and Peppermint faces me again.

"Now, what happened?"

So fucking much.

"What happened is your president took a nosedive off her already wobbly rocker."

Peppermint's eyes widen, but then she laughs. "She flipped the script, didn't she?"

"That's what she said. Now what the hell does it mean?"

"Ask her."

"I tried!"

Peppermint hitches a thumb over her shoulder. "She went that way. My guess is she headed straight for the targets. That's usually where she goes when she's upset."

I move to step around her, but her hand on my arm stops me.

"Harlow's not always as tough as she wants people to think," she says. "Just… give her a chance to explain. It might take her a hot minute to get the words out, but she'll get them out one way or another."

"Yeah, I will. Thanks."

Peppermint nods and lets go of my arm. I remain there.

"I'm sorry about last night," I say to her. "I reacted to what you said and… I'm sorry."

Again, Peppermint nods. "Follow the path through the trees until you come to a clearing. That's where she'll be."

She walks away, leaving me to stride through the main room of the clubhouse toward the door with the 'exit' sign above it. I go where Peppermint instructed, over the path and through the trees, but I stop when I see Harlow sitting on a log.

Harlow isn't alone, so I stay quiet, hidden, and shamelessly listen in on her conversation.

CHAPTER 19

Harlow

"I DON'T KNOW whether to be proud of you or disappointed."

Shame like I've never felt before crashes over me like a waterfall. Ever since my mom died, Tahiti has been my biggest supporter, a surrogate mother in a way. And to hear that something I've done might be disappointing to her fills me to a miserable degree.

"It wasn't supposed to happen like it did. If I thought for one second that he'd actually kill his father, I never would've done it."

"Why didn't you just stick to the plan you gave him?"

I shrug. "I was flipping the script," I say, sounding small, almost childish. Other than Peppermint, Tahiti is the only person I'll open up to like this, let my guard down around. Right now, she's not my club sister. She's my friend.

"And where the fuck did you get the idea to do that?"

I stare at the ground and bite my tongue. Unfortunately, that's all the answer Tahiti needs.

"Pepper." It's not a question. "I swear you guys are two pieces of the same crumbling pie."

"It's not her fault," I say defensively.

"Didn't say it was."

"You should've heard him, T. He yelled at me, said I betrayed him."

"You did."

"Ouch."

"It's the truth, Har." Tahiti takes a deep breath. "What I don't get is why. You had him where you wanted him, under your thumb where you could keep an eye on him. It didn't matter if you could trust him because he was never going to be out of your sight. You held all the cards."

"It's not that simple," I mumble, not wanting to have to explain myself.

"It is that simple," she insists.

When she pauses, I make the mistake of looking at her. Which means she can look at me too and see exactly what I didn't want her or anyone else to see.

"Ah, now I understand." Tahiti smiles and for a moment, I imagine she *is* my mom. Because I could really use my mom right about now. "You like him."

"No. He's the enemy."

"Is he though? Because he just killed his father and got you out of the path of flying bullets. And after you *flipped the script*. He didn't have to do that. Honestly, I'm surprised you're still breathing at all. He's probably programmed to retaliate for any betrayal. You got lucky if you ask me."

"Yeah, well, I didn't ask you," I grumble. "Why is everyone on his side all of a sudden?"

"Because we're on the outside looking in, Har. It's easier for us to analyze and see alternative explanations for things. You, on the other hand, are too close, and are only using past experiences and pain to fuel your actions." Tahiti rests her hand on my knee. "And I'm on your side. I'm *always* on your side."

She pushes herself up, kisses the top of my head, and then

moves around the log to head toward the clubhouse. I think I'm alone, but then I hear her speak to someone.

"Oh man, what I wouldn't give to stay and watch the fireworks." Tahiti's chuckle floats in the air to me. "But I think I'll let you two talk for a while."

I'll kill whoever sent him out here.

The only person she could be talking to, saying that to, is Malachi. And I'm not in the mood for Malachi and his yelling right now.

"This seat taken?"

"Not now, Malachi."

"Not your call, Harlow," he counters and sits down on the log.

"I thought we agreed that everything is my call."

"Yeah, we did. Then you decided to go rogue."

I huff out a breath and push myself up to stand. I pick my hatchet up off the ground where it had been sitting at my feet and move to the throwing line.

For the next ten minutes, I throw that thing at the target like my life depends on it. And Malachi sits there quietly, watching.

"You about done?" he finally asks.

"Not even close."

"That's okay. I'll wait."

And the fucker does. He sits there for the next half hour while I work out all the junk clogging up my brain. But throwing my hatchet is tiring and even I'm cognizant of when it becomes unsafe for me to keep pushing myself.

It's become unsafe. I walk to the target and yank my blade out of the wood to carry it back toward the throwing line. I stare at the empty space on the log next to Malachi, debating on whether or not I want to be that close to him. I decide against it and drop to the ground instead.

"The ground it is then." Malachi moves from the log to sit in front of me in the dirt.

"What do you want from me, Malachi?"

"I want to know what the hell happened today."

"You know what happened," I snap. I drag my fingertip through the dirt lazily so I have something other than him to focus on. "You were there, same as me."

"Anyone ever tell you that you're stubborn?"

"Yep."

"Jesus," he clips out. "Will you fucking look at me?"

I continue to watch my finger in the dirt until he grips my chin and forces my face up so my eyes meet his.

"Talk to me," he pleads and drops his hand. "Please."

Hearing the desperation snaps something in me and I break.

"What the fuck do you want me to say, Malachi?" I shout. "That I fucked up? Fine, I fucked up. Do you want me to explain to you that I wasn't honest with you about the plan because I needed to see how you'd react? To figure out if I could trust you? Fine, I wasn't honest because I made the unilateral decision to do whatever it took to determine if you could be trusted." The more I talk, the louder I get. "Do you wanna hear about how I'm ashamed of what I did? Great, I'm goddamn ashamed. And let's not forget about my feelings. Is that what you want me to talk about? That I have feelings for you? That, regardless of everything I thought to be true and right in my life doesn't feel true and right anymore. That even though we have been on opposing teams for the last decade, I like you and don't want to be your enemy. Is that what you wanna fucking hear?!"

"Is it the truth?"

"Yes, goddammit!"

"Then yeah, that's what I want to hear."

My entire being seems to deflate, everything I have left inside me, gone.

"What are we even doing, Malachi?"

"What do you mean?"

"We keep going round and round. It's the same conversation every time one of us opens our mouth. We don't trust each other. We're enemies. We both have reasons for our actions, but we aren't willing to share them. Yada, yada, yada."

Malachi is quiet for a moment, and I start to think he's not going to say anything. But then he draws his knees up and wraps his arms around them.

"Her name was Mina."

CHAPTER 20
Malachi

HER NAME WAS MINA.

I let those words ruminate in my mind for a minute, almost as if testing myself to see if the world will come crashing down around me at having said them out loud. I never intended to tell Harlow about Mina. Never expected to *want* to tell her. Yet here we are.

I don't know what Harlow expected to hear come out of my mouth but judging by her wide eyes and the way her lips are parted, it wasn't another woman's name.

I take a deep breath and force myself to tell Harlow all of my reasons for doing what I did. It'll either ease her mind or send her running. No matter what, there's no turning back now.

"I was eighteen when I met her, she was seventeen. I'd just moved out of my father's house and into a place of my own. I saw her on the boardwalk one night when I was hanging out with my cousin, Nicholi." I watch Harlow for her reactions to every word I'm saying. "He was the younger guy at my father's earlier. Anyway, we were trolling for girls as usual. And there she was, in line at the ice cream shop. I was sunk the second I laid eyes on her. I introduced myself and asked her out. We went on a date the next weekend and became inseparable from that night."

"You loved her."

"In my way, yes. I knew my father could never know about her, not with the business he ran, the trafficking." Harlow's sharp inhale cuts through me, but I force myself to continue. "I didn't even tell Nicholi that we went on a date because I knew he couldn't keep his mouth shut. He's always wanted to impress our fathers. Mina and I dated for two years before we were found out."

I tip my head back and stare up at the sky, watch the clouds shift above us for a minute while I choose my next words.

"Something you need to know about me, Harlow, is that I used to be as vile as my father. I knew about the sex trafficking. Hell, I helped with the exchanges, with setting up the stash houses where we'd keep everyone in between procurement and sales, and then working shifts at those houses to watch over everyone. It never really bothered me because it's all I knew."

Disgust flashes in her green eyes. Even though I know I deserve it, it doesn't make it hurt any less. She's the one person on this Earth that I don't want to disgust. Not her, never her.

"What changed?" she asks.

I let out a humorless laugh. "Everything. Nothing." I shrug.

"I don't understand."

"Nothing changed. My father did what he always did. He found out about Mina and had her taken after her shift at a local restaurant in Ocean City. I was supposed to pick her up that night, but Nicholi called with some bullshit about needing help with something. It was all a ruse to keep me away. But in typical Nicholi fashion, he blabbed and told me what was going on. I confronted my father about it that night, but it didn't matter. He already had a buyer lined up, but even if he hadn't, I couldn't have saved her."

Tears brim in Harlow's eyes, but she remains quiet.

"Mina knew all about my father. I never kept that from her. But I promised her she'd be safe as long as he didn't know about us." I press a fist to my chest to ease the ache that thinking about how I failed Mina always brings. "My father assigned me to the stash house she was in. I'd talk to her when no one else from the family was there. I wanted to break her out, but I couldn't. She begged me to free her, to run away with her, and I agreed. We planned it out to the last detail."

"So you kept your promise."

"I tried. Fuck, I tried to keep it. We made it as far as the New Jersey state line crossing into Pennsylvania before he caught up to us. Loaded us both up into a van and dragged us back to the stash house. No one said a word the entire time. He let me out of the van when we got there, told me to go inside and take care of our product. I defied him then. My first act of defiance that was in his face. I reached out to help Mina out of the van, and he put a bullet in her head before our hands even touched."

"Oh my God," she whispers.

"Like I said, nothing had changed. My father was always going to be what he was. It didn't matter who he hurt along the way or the trail of devastation he left in his wake. And that realization changed everything. I vowed right then and there that I was done. I would do whatever it took to take out my father and those who support him, and stop the trafficking."

I stop talking for a minute as I recall the emotions that swept over me that night. I remember feeling like my life couldn't possibly get any worse, like a part of me died right along with Mina. And I suppose a part of me *did* die, the part

I was happy to say goodbye to, the part of me I learned to hate.

"A week after Mina died, there was an exchange scheduled. It was a new buyer so there were a lot of unknowns. I refused to go. I wanted nothing to do with what was going down. So my father took my little brother, Mortichi, in my place. My brother was sixteen. Just a kid. Sure, he'd been to exchanges before, that's how we lived, but he always stayed in the background. Not this time. Fuck, I remember Mortichi's excitement. Idiot drove to my place that afternoon to thank me for growing a conscience because he was finally getting his chance to show our father what he could do. He idolized our father. We got into an argument because I tried to talk him out of going, tried to convince him that this life would suck his soul out of his body and spit it out, bloody and broken. He laughed in my face and left. The next time I saw him it was from a distance at his funeral because I wasn't permitted to attend. I had to wear a fucking disguise to my own brother's funeral so my father wouldn't know I was there."

Unable to sit still any longer, I rise to my feet and begin to pace. Beams of sunlight filter through the trees, almost ethereal in the way they slash through the air. There's a breeze and my cheeks are cold, which is odd considering the warm temperature. I rub my hands over them to warm them up, and when I pull them away, they're wet. That's when I realize I've been silently crying.

I guess I never knew just how much I kept bottled inside until this very moment. I've let out the anger over the years, but never the sadness. I've used my rage to fuel my every decision, but kept the heartbreak locked away.

Until now. Until Harlow.

"My mother killed Mortichi."

My feet become rooted to the ground like the trees

surrounding us. I take a deep breath before yanking the roots and walking to stand in front of Harlow.

"I know."

Harlow looks up at me, shock written in the creases of her face. "Then why'd you come to me? Of all the people you could go to for help to take out your father, to stop the trafficking, why the Devil's Handmaidens?"

"Because I knew you'd help," I say simply. "I couldn't go to the police. I had too much blood on my hands for that. Maybe not literal blood, but I wasn't innocent. Even if I could've gone to the police, it wouldn't have changed anything. Sure, maybe my father would've gotten arrested, but then what? Either he continues to run the operations from a jail cell or my Uncle Angelo, his brother, takes over. Neither option was one I could live with." I squat down to be at eye level with her. "I came to you because I knew what your club does. I knew that, when it comes to sex trafficking, you can accomplish what no one else can. My partner and I sp—"

"Your partner?" she asks with a narrow glare.

Fuck.

I run my hand through my hair as I lower myself to sit fully. I hadn't intended to tell her about him. Until this is all over, no one can know he's involved. It's not safe.

You've trusted her so far.

That thought runs through my head on a loop. I have trusted her so far. I've had to. And aside from the shit show this morning, which oddly enough, I understand, she hasn't given me reason not to.

Then why stop now?

"Yes, my partner."

I take a deep breath, hold it so long my head starts to swim before releasing it.

Here goes nothing.

"Nico, Nicholi's twin brother, has been helping me from afar."

"Nicholi's twin brother? How did I not know he had a twin?" Harlow's expression hardens, but I don't get the sense that her anger is directed at me. No, there's something in her tone, something more along the lines of anger at… herself? "I've gone through the information my mom had on your family. Dozens of times. And I don't remember seeing anything about Nicholi having a twin brother, not once."

"Good to know."

"What?"

"Nico is what you'd call the black sheep of the family. Like me, he despises what our family does, what the Ricci name stands for. Nico was more interested in computers and code than he was in girls and the family business. He's a fucking genius with that shit." A memory flashes and I chuckle. "I remember when he was thirteen, he wrote a computer code that corrupted all of my father's files, the ones he thought no one knew about. Dates, times, locations, contacts… you name it, it was in those files. It wasn't hard to figure out who did it. Especially when your twin is the family nark. Nico was beat and forced to correct what he fucked up. Then he was shipped off to a boarding school under a different name and erased from the family tree."

"Jesus."

"I tried to find him, but I was only fourteen and had nowhere near his talent for tech. I'd given up on him until he reached out to me after Mina. Turns out, he'd been tracking the family's every move. All of that information I gave you came from him."

"But I thought…"

"What, that I'd gathered all of it?" I laugh. "Hardly. I'm in charge of Umbria's Universe and the escort service we run out of there, but that's it. To outsiders, I'm an important figure. I mean, how would it look if the son of the don was exiled? Gotta uphold that public image." I wave my hand like it's no big deal. "On the inside though, I might as well have been banished, same as Nico. I don't have access to anything that isn't important to the casino and escort business. I'm given just enough to make everything appear copacetic. And my father continues to pull the strings and test my loyalty every chance he gets."

"Are there others like you, like Nico?"

"What do you mean?"

"Is there anyone else who isn't exactly loyal to the family, who would help us?"

"Us?"

Harlow's eyes lock on mine for a moment before she reaches out and threads her fingers through mine.

Fuck, this feels good. This feels right.

"Yeah, Malachi, us," she confirms. "You came to me for help, and I told you I'd help you."

I nod, emotion clogging my throat. I really believed that once all of my secrets were out in the open, she'd run. Tell me to fuck off and figure out my family drama myself. But she's not.

And that means more than I can say.

"There are a few. Not as many as I'd like though. Nico helps as much as he can from a distance, but he can't be here in the thick of things. And then there's Gill. I'm sure you remember him."

"How could I forget?"

"Right. Well, he works for me, not my father. I brought him in, and he's loyal to me. There's about ten more, give or take." I shake my head. "But I'm not sure it matters anymore."

"Why?"

"Harlow, I killed my father. It's no longer a numbers game, no longer about who has the most people on their side to fight with them. I wanted a war, and I'm gonna get it. Only, instead of being a beacon of hope for those who want things to change in the family, I'm public enemy number one. Uncle

Angelo and Nicholi will be gunning for me, as will every single other person loyal to my father."

I stare at her, intently.

"You asked me this morning if I was willing to die for my endgame, and I told you I was. But I proved it to you when I slit my father's throat and chose you over them."

CHAPTER 21

Harlow

WOW.

I don't even know what to say to Malachi after everything he's told me. And really, what is there to say? He's the physical embodiment of the saying 'don't judge a book by its cover'. I thought I had him pegged, but I was wrong.

I fucking hate being wrong.

Rather than address every single thing he's revealed to me, I settle on, "What now?"

"I don't know. I was kinda hoping you'd have the answer to that."

Right. Because this is our thing, my thing.

"Well, I think the first thing we need to do is fill my sisters in on everything. They need to know what they're really up against, who they're fighting for."

"No."

"No?"

Malachi shakes his head. "No. They don't need to know my business."

"Yeah, they do. We don't have to give them all the details, but they deserve to know the basics. Think about it, Malachi. Take your pride and emotions out of it and you'll see I'm right. They need to be able to trust you, to understand you if they're going to fight for you."

"Isn't fighting to save the victims enough? Isn't stopping the trafficking enough?"

It always has been.

"Honestly? Yes, it's enough. But…"

But what?

I like this man more than I should, or more than I thought I should. I want to tell him, to explain to him that, despite only a few days having passed, he's important to me. He matters. But how do you explain to someone that you care for them and nothing can ever come of it? How do you tell them that you want to be with them, that it's as if your soul recognized theirs on some level that goes beyond the boundaries of what is explainable, and yet, you can't act on it because three words in the English language are impossible for you?

How the fuck do you look a man in the eyes and tell them that you are incapable of giving them what they deserve?

You just do. Because he spilled his guts to you and now it's your turn.

"But?" Malachi prompts when I get lost in thought.

"But making it more personal will fuel them."

"And knowing more about me will make it more personal?"

"Yes. No." I shake my head. "Fuck, this is harder than I thought."

"Take your time, *bella*. No rush."

Malachi's patience is gonna be the death of me.

"I like you," I spit out.

His lips twitch. "Pretty sure we established that when you were yelling at me."

Oh, right. I forgot about my little outburst. Not surprising, though, with everything he's divulged.

"If my sisters get to know you, the real you and not the

public persona of you, then maybe they'll understand and be more accepting of the fact that I like you."

"Okay. But I don't think you're giving them enough credit."

"What?"

"I've seen you with them, seen the way they respect you. I get the sense that if I'm important to you, I'm important to them. Isn't that how family works?"

"Well, yes."

"So, it stands to reason that if you give them the information they must have in order to move forward, that coupled with the fact that I'm important to you will make them fight as hard as they've ever fought. Because being a part of your inner circle makes me a part of theirs. And it's that way because that's family."

"Since when did you become the expert on family?" I snark. "You've had a shit example."

Malachi chuckles at me. "True, my family is shit. But I understand family, Harlow. I know how they're supposed to work. I know how I'll raise my children to regard family. It's not a difficult concept, just not one I'm used to."

"You want children?"

"Yeah, someday."

"So you want a family of your own?"

"Isn't that what I just said?"

Panic claws at me from the inside out. This is why I shouldn't have told him I like him. This is why nothing can come from whatever is between us.

"I can't give you that."

"I didn't ask you to."

I frantically shake my head. "No, you don't get it." I scramble to my feet and cross my arms over my chest, as if that will protect my heart. "I don't do relationships. We may like each other, but that's all it can ever be. Dust particles of feelings that get swept under the rug, never to see the light of day again."

Malachi stands and rests his hands on my shoulders.

"Explain," he commands, but there's no heat in his tone.

"I've had relationships, Malachi. And they always end the same, with them wanting more than I'm capable of giving. I can't..." I swallow past the lump in my throat. "The last person I tried to say 'I love you' to was my mom, and she died. The night the treaty was signed, I got out the words 'I love' before she was out the door. I never finished telling her. I don't even know if she heard me. And I'll never know because she sacrificed herself so I'd have a better life. She gave herself up because she loved me so damn much, but I couldn't even finish telling her how I felt."

Tears are streaming down my face, and Malachi swipes them away with his thumbs.

"Since that night, I've never been able to say it to another person. I've tried. But I can't get the words out. It's like a force stronger than me makes it impossible."

"But there are people you love."

"Of course there are. Peppermint, Tahiti, and the rest of my sisters. I love them so much it hurts. But I've never told them."

"I'm sure they know how you feel. Saying the words isn't what makes love real. It's in your actions."

"You're missing the point."

"Maybe, but I still think you need to hear what I said. Words alone are just words. Anyone can say 'I love you'. But it's in a person's actions where you really see the love, where you feel it."

"You're annoying, you know that?"

Malachi smirks. "You've said something to that affect a time or two."

He moves my arms to my sides and pulls me close. I

should stop him, but I don't. Instead, I soak up what he's offering. I soak it up because it could be the last time I can.

Resting his chin on my head, Malachi asks, "What would happen if you told someone you loved them and meant it?"

"Nothing, I suppose. But people die, they leave you or die, and I don't want to feel that pain again. I don't want to open myself up like that. It's not worth it."

"Ah, *bella.* You're so wrong. It is worth it. Love is always worth it."

"Was loving Mina worth it?"

The minute the words are out, I want to call them back, but it's too late. Malachi stiffens. I wrap my arms around his waist, and, after a second, he relaxes on a sigh.

"There was a time I would've said no. She's dead because of me. But now?" I feel his head bob above me. "Yeah, loving her was worth it. I wouldn't trade the two years we had together for anything. And when I forget that, all I have to do is look at you."

I step back and look into his eyes. "What? Why?"

"Because I like you, Harlow. I really fucking like you." I open my mouth to protest, to reiterate all the reasons I just gave him as to why he shouldn't, but he places a finger over my lips. "I can't change how I feel. I like you and we're gonna see where this goes. I'm not asking for love. You'll give me that when you're ready. But as for Mina? Yeah, loving her was worth it. Losing her was worth all the pain and heartbreak because it led me to you. Every second of my life was worth it for me to be exactly where I am right now. I'd die for you. I wouldn't for her. But you?" Malachi nods. "I'd die for you a thousand times over."

"But why? We barely—"

"Don't overthink it, Harlow. Neither of us can really explain what we feel, so why try? We don't have to put labels on it. It is what it is. I like you and you like me, and for now, that's enough."

Is it?

Maybe Malachi is right. Maybe it is enough. Then again, maybe not. But one thing is for certain: no amount of feelings will be enough if he's dead. So for now, I can accept the fact that we like each other and are apparently going to see where this goes. And while we do that, I'll fight to the death to keep him alive.

You're willing to die for him.

Holy. Fucking. Shit!

CHAPTER 22

Malachi

IT'S NOT EVEN four in the afternoon, and I'm exhausted. When I woke up this morning, I thought I'd be meeting with my father and then… Well, I didn't know what would come next. But I definitely didn't imagine that it would be what actually transpired.

Murder, escape, emotional rollercoasters… Like I said, exhausted.

"I really need to get back inside."

I nod at Harlow.

"Go ahead," I tell her. "I need to call Nico. Fill him in."

I pull my cell out of my pocket and turn it on. I'd turned it off before going into my father's house this morning and forgot all about it. When it's on, notification after notification fills up the screen.

"Fuck!" I roar.

"What?" Harlow snatches my phone from my hand and looks at the screen. "Damn." She hands it back. "You deal with that. I'm gonna call church and fill my sisters in."

I open up my texting app to read the messages from Nico.

How did it go this morning?

Mal, why are you ignoring me?

What's going on?

Those are all time stamped within an hour of when I should've been done with the meeting with my father. The next text is time stamped thirty minutes later, and there's several that follow in quick succession.

What the fuck happened?

That wasn't the plan!

Answer your phone, Mal!

CALL ME!

I guess the cat is out of the bag. I close out the texts and tap on Nico's phone number. Sitting on the log, I brace myself to get yelled at, again.

"Where the fuck have you been?" Nico asks.

"Hello to you too."

"Don't start with me," he barks. "You were only supposed to *meet* with Antonio, Mal, not kill him!"

"His death was always the goal, Nico," I remind him. "His, Angelo's, and Nicholi's. I just sped things up a bit."

"You didn't just speed them up. You added nitrous to that shit." Nico sighs. "At least tell me you had no choice."

My pause is the only answer he needs.

"Motherfucker," he says harshly. "What happened? And don't leave anything out. Because you text me that chick's plan this morning, and so far, I haven't heard anything that even comes close to resembling it."

"She changed everything up. Told my father she was accepting my offer to buy Devil's Double Down."

"Okay, that doesn't explain why you killed him."

"Harlow threw me under the bus, Nico. Came right out and said that she wanted my father to call off the war he was going to start."

"Fucking bitch!"

Lava hot fury flows through my veins at that. "Watch it," I snarl. "She did what she had to do."

"I can't be hearing this right. She basically told Antonio that you betrayed him by telling her about the war, and you're defending her? She's painted a giant red target on your back, Malachi."

"I know. She has. They're gonna be gunning for me. But she did it to see if I could be trusted."

"And you killing your father proved that to her?"

"Yes." I laugh, but there's no humor in it. "I didn't even hesitate, Nico. I didn't go in there planning on killing him, but in that moment, I knew it's what I had to do. I knew Harlow must have had a reason for not telling me the real plan, and I went with my gut. Then I got us the fuck out of there."

"Dammit."

"What?"

"I want to be mad as hell at you. I want to fly to New Jersey and kick your sorry ass. But I can't. This chick obviously means something to you. You're sucking all the fun out of this for me."

"Sorry, cousin." I shrug even though he can't see me. "What can I say? She's… special."

"Special, huh?"

"Yeah."

And just like that, the argument is over. Like I explained to Harlow, it's how family works. Real family.

"So what do we do now? You can't exactly take out the rest of them after this. They'll kill you before you get within a mile of them."

"I don't know yet. Harlow's meeting with her club now, and I assume they'll come up with a plan."

"Wait. They're meeting about all of this, about your fate, and you're not there?"

"I wasn't exactly invited. We know enough about MCs to know how they operate and including outsiders in their meetings isn't something they do."

"I wouldn't exactly call you an outsider."

"You know what I mean."

"Malachi, you are not this soft. This is your life we're talking about. I don't care what feelings you have for her, don't give up your balls."

"What do you want me to do?" I counter. "Storm into the room and demand to be a part of their planning?"

"Yes!" he shouts. "That's exactly what I want you to do. Listen, I'm stuck here in the middle of fucking nowhere. I can't do it myself, so you have to."

"She'll kick my ass."

"I've read her stats, man. She's a buck twenty soaking wet. I doubt she'll do any real damage."

An image of Gill flashes through my mind, cut up and bruised.

"Harlow carries a hatchet, Nico."

Shit, I have gone soft.

"You're afraid of her."

It's a statement, not a question.

"No."

And I'm not. I don't think. Okay, maybe a little. Harlow is dangerous and I don't want to be on her bad side. Not when we're finally on the same side.

"Malachi Ricci, future king of the Familia, is afraid of a biker chick." Nico laughs hysterically. I fail to see the humor. "Oh shit. This is good."

"Stuff it, asshole," I snap, getting more than a little pissed at his teasing.

"No. Nope, not happening. I know we haven't seen each other in a decade, but the boy I knew wouldn't have backed down because he was scared. Are you telling me that the man you are will?"

"No."

"Then walk your ass to wherever the fuck their meeting is and join it."

"Fine."

I don't know why I'm listening to him, why I'm letting him goad me into doing this, but I am. I walk through the trees and down the path toward the back door, phone still in hand, call still connected.

"I so wish I could see this in person," Nico says.

I ignore him and let my frustration with him fuel my actions. I stride through the door and down the hall to the DHMC meeting room.

"I'm here," I tell him.

"You're just standing outside the door, aren't you?" he asks.

"Fucking hell, how do you know this shit?"

"I know all," he taunts. "Knock on the door, Malachi. It's easy, you just lift your hand…"

I tune him out and lift my arm. I hesitate for a minute before knocking on the door.

And then I brace myself.

CHAPTER 23

Harlow

"AM I HEARING THIS RIGHT? Because he experienced a tragedy and had a sudden change of heart, we're supposed to forgive everything he's done and everything his family stands for?"

I just finished giving my sisters as many details about Malachi's past as they need. I explained about him losing Mina, about his cousin and brother. I walked them through all of his reasons for wanting to take out his family and put an end to the trafficking.

"No, Spooks," I say to our SAA. "I'm not saying you have to forgive him or his family. I just need you all to understand his motives."

"His motives don't make him a good guy, Prez," Spooks counters.

"You're right," Peppermint says before I can speak.

Which is good because I want to argue with Spooks, but I know that won't get me anywhere. I've always prided myself on being a solid MC president, of leading my sisters and always having their backs, no matter what. I'd die for them. And I've done all of that while making sure they felt like they could speak their mind, without consequence… to a degree. Right now, Spooks is testing me though.

"Motives aren't the measure of a man," Peppermint continues. "But I don't think you're really listening, Spooks. I don't think you're really hearing Harlow, really hearing what she's *not* saying."

Spooks stares at me, her face hard. She's scrutinizing me, searching for the words that I left unspoken. I see the moment it clicks because her eyes widen a fraction of a second before she slumps in her chair.

"Shit," Spooks mutters.

"Dammit, Prez," Mama says.

"Never thought I'd see the day," Giggles adds.

"It's about fucking time," Tahiti huffs out.

"How do you want me to write this in the notes, Prez?" Story asks, laughter in her tone. "Or should I leave out all the feelings for the enemy turned love interest stuff?"

"Okay, okay, cut it out," I snap, uncomfortable with their ribbing.

Spooks raises her hand, and I roll my eyes.

"We're not in kindergarten, bitch," I spit out. "Just say what you want to say."

Spooks sits up and leans on the table. "First, I'm not a bitch." Everyone laughs and Spooks grins. "Second, if you like the guy, you shoulda just started with that. He matters to you, he matters to us. You fight for him, we fight for him. It's as simple as that, Prez."

Malachi was right. Although I won't ever admit that to him.

"I appreciate that." I take a deep breath. "And yes, he matters to me. So, now that he's got a target on his back, how do we—"

The knock on the door has me narrowing my eyes. No one interrupts church, and everyone knows that. So who the fuck is at the door?

"Enter," I call out angrily, fully prepared to verbally rip apart whoever it is.

The door swings open and Malachi steps in, a sheepish look on his face.

"Aw, fuck," Peppermint mumbles under her breath.

"What the fuck do you think you're doing?" I snap at Malachi.

"Is that her? It sounds like her, or what I imagine she sounds like anyway. Harlow Monroe, badass biker bitch."

Malachi lifts his hand and shakes his cell. "Harlow, meet Nico, my cousin. Nico, yes, that's Harlow."

"You can't be in here," I say through gritted teeth.

"Don't get mad at him," Nico says. "I goaded him into interrupting. My cousin seems to have misplaced his balls where you're concerned."

Laughs erupt around the table, but I hold a fist up and they go silent. As for Malachi, his knuckles are white from how hard he's gripping his cell.

"I assure you, I've done nothing with his balls. The fact remains, this meeting is closed."

"Pity," Nico says, sounding sad. "The balls are the gateway to bliss. Well, maybe not the gateway, but they're pretty important in the grand scheme of things. Sexually. I'm talking about sex, just in case you hadn't picked up on that."

Malachi groans.

And I can't help but snicker. As inappropriate as this is, I like Nico.

I lock eyes with Malachi, unable to hide my grin. "I thought you said he was a genius?"

"Aw, Mal, you said that?" Nico asks. "You really think I'm a genius?"

Malachi holds the phone close to his mouth. "I'm gonna kill you when you come back, Nico," he growls. "I swear to God I am."

"Nah, you won't do that. You love me." Nico clears his

throat. "Besides, we've worked too hard to make sure I can come home. We haven't seen each other in a decade, so no, you won't kill me. Unless you squeeze me too hard. Because you're gonna hug me, cousin. I know you are."

Time to reign this back in. I could listen to them banter all day, but there's too much to do.

"Nico, as much fun as this has been," I start. "Did you have a reason for goading Malachi to interrupt my meeting? Or did you just want to get him in trouble?"

"I have a reason." Playful Nico is gone. The Nico I'm hearing now sounds more like what I'm used to with Ricci's. "I know what happened this morning, and the powers that be are not happy. The general consensus is that Malachi should be taken out, although there are a few who disagree. And I want to know what you plan to do about it. Since it was your actions that signed his death warrant."

"Nico," Malachi admonishes, much like you would a child. "I told you, she—"

"I can speak for myself, Malachi." He shuts his mouth. "Nico, I know what I did wasn't according to plan, but I didn't force Malachi to kill his father. He did that all on his own."

"He did it for you."

"And that was his choice."

"I'm right here," Malachi clips out.

"Shut up," Nico and I bark simultaneously.

"All of you, shut up!" Peppermint shouts and rises from her chair. I stare at my VP. "None of this matters. Yes, Harlow changed the plan. Maybe she shouldn't have, but it's done. And yes, Malachi killed his father. We can argue all day long about the whys, but it doesn't matter. That's between Malachi and Harlow. Right now, we need to focus on how we're gonna keep Malachi safe and put an end to the trafficking. That's it."

Peppermint huffs out a breath and through the speaker of Malachi's cell I hear faint clapping.

"Mi sposerai e avrai i miei bambini?"

"What?" Peppermint asks and looks at Malachi. "What did he just say?"

"Uh…" Malachi looks at me. I arch a brow, daring him to translate for his cousin. "He asked you to marry him and have his babies."

Peppermint drops back into her chair, her face draining of color. "I will never marry a Ricci," she says vehemently. "Never."

Malachi's expression registers his confusion, and I give him a slight shake of my head. I know why Peppermint feels that way, but that's her story to tell, not mine.

"It was a joke," Nico says and then, clearly not knowing when to shut the fuck up, he tacks on, "For now."

"Bad joke, cousin."

"Yeah, I'm getting that," Nico agrees. "Sorry."

"Can we get back to figuring out how we're gonna fix this?" Giggles asks, frustration written on her face. "I promised Noah I'd watch a movie with him tonight, since we're stuck on partial lockdown."

"As soon as Malachi leaves, we can get back to our regularly scheduled programming."

"I'm not leaving," Malachi argues.

"Excuse me?"

"You heard him," Nico says. "He's not leaving."

I settle my hand over the handle of my hatchet at my waist.

"Remember me telling you she has a hatchet?" Malachi says into the phone.

"Uh, yeah," Nico responds.

"I'm leaving the room now. And I'm hanging up the phone. I'll—"

"Wait," I bark. "Nico, you seem to have your hands in

everything and know all. How much time do we have to plan? How long until they come for Malachi?"

"Not long. They'll bury Antonio first. That order has already come down the pipeline. As soon as he's in the ground, you've got a week, at most. Funeral is scheduled for six days from now."

"How in the hell did they get it scheduled already?" Spooks asks. "That shit takes time."

"Not for the Ricci's," Nico says, resignation in his tone.

"What about the trafficking? When's the next time anything transpires as far as that's concerned?"

"Two weeks from now. Uncle Angelo shifted the schedule around when he initially ordered the war to start. All the stash houses are empty, cleared out with the last exchange. Procurement is still going on though. Those never stop."

"Thanks, Nico," I say.

"You can thank me by keeping my cousin alive."

"I'll call you later," Malachi tells him before disconnecting the call.

He shoves his phone into his pocket. His head swivels to take in the club members around the table as he backpedals toward the door. "Sorry for the interruption." His gaze locks on mine. "I'll be at the bar."

And with that, Malachi disappears into the hallway, pulling the door shut behind him.

"Prez?"

I glance at Mama, who's been quiet for almost the entire time.

"Yeah?"

"I don't think your life is ever going to be boring."

The entire room breaks out into ruckus laughter, me included.

CHAPTER 24

Malachi

AS I ENTER the main room at the clubhouse, my mind races. What the fuck is wrong with me? I'm a leader, not a follower. I'm strong, decisive, in control. Unless Harlow's around.

There's no room for soft in the Ricci family.

My father's words taunt me. I've always done what was expected of me, done what I had to in order to satisfy the puppet master. Hell, when I started this whole thing with Harlow, the puppet b*ecame* the puppet master.

And for what? To please a man who I despise? To be something I'm not? I can't lie and say that I don't like having control. I do. It's in my DNA. But I'm learning that I don't always *have* to have control.

There's a difference.

A difference that's pointed out to me, time and time again. Every decision of Harlow's that I follow, every choice I make to trust her and let her lead, I give up control. It isn't a bad thing.

It's different. Which is exactly what I've been fighting for this last decade. Something different. Something I can be proud of.

There's absolutely room for soft in the Ricci family, old man.

There is. Because I say there is. I can step back and let Harlow be the woman she wants to be, the president of DHMC, and I won't question her decisions. I also know that, if the roles were reversed and it was me making decisions about my organization, she'd step back and let me make them.

We're the same, Harlow and me. Both trying to figure out how to be two sides to the same coin and then melding those two coins together to make the perfect piece of jewelry.

Jesus, that's corny. I am soft.

And that's okay.

"There's also the damn hatchet," I mutter to myself.

"Talkin' to yourself is a sure sign that you need a drink."

Lost in thought, I hadn't noticed that I'd made it to the bar. Shaking my head to clear it, I look at the woman who spoke. She's staring at me with a grin.

"What?"

"You were talkin' to yourself," she says. "If you're to the point where that's happenin', alcohol is a must."

"Oh, right." I peruse the liquor bottles on the shelf behind the bar. "Whiskey, neat. Please."

"Darlin', this isn't those fancy bars I'm sure you're used to," she drawls, nodding toward my chest. I glance down and see that I'm still in my suit, although it's bloody and disheveled. "No need to stand on ceremony here."

She goes to make my drink, and when she sets it in front of me, I bring it to my lips and down it in one gulp.

"Well, now, that was fast. Another?"

I nod. "Keep 'em coming."

"Sure thing, darlin'."

I drink the second whiskey a little more leisurely. "What's your name?" I ask her.

"Fiona."

"Nice to meet you, Fiona. I'm Malachi."

"I know who you are," she tells me, winking. "You've had the club in an uproar the last few days."

"Right."

"So, you said somethin' about a hatchet."

"Huh?"

"When you were talkin' to yourself, you said 'there's also the damn hatchet'. Since my Prez is the only one who carries that particular weapon at all times, I assume you were grumblin' about her."

"You're a member of the club?" I ask her, deflecting her question.

Fiona points to a patch on her cut, and I notice the diamond sparkling on her ring finger. "Prospect."

"And your husband doesn't mind?"

"'Course not." She chuckles as she refills my glass. "He'd be a hypocrite if he did. Coast is the VP of his own club."

"How does that work, exactly? From what I've seen, dominance seems to be a pretty consistent personality trait among MC members."

Fiona throws her head back and laughs. Once she calms, she leans forward and rests her elbows on the bar.

"It works just fine. The harder part for us is the fact that his club is law enforcement and DHMC is, well, not always law abiding."

"Damn," I whistle out.

"Yeah. That can get squirrely at times. But Coast and me, we make it work. It's what you do when you love someone."

Love? No one said anything about love.

"I know you didn't ask, but I'm going to give you a piece of advice." Fiona cups her hand around the corner of her mouth like she's about to divulge a national secret. "Tell her to bring the hatchet to bed."

Bring the hatchet to—

The idea takes root in my brain, and the more I allow it to grow, the harder *I* grow.

"I promise you, two dominant personalities can work, darlin'," Fiona says, straightening from the bar top and glancing past me. "You just have to want it bad enough."

"Have to want what bad enough?"

I whip my head around and see Harlow standing behind me. My eyes drop to the leather wrapped handle at her waist and my cock swells.

"Business handled?" I ask curtly.

"Yeah, for now. Why?"

I turn and lift the tumbler off the bar to down the last of my whiskey before standing from my stool. Grabbing Harlow's hand, I drag her toward the stairs to the second floor.

"Malachi, what are you doing?" Harlow asks. "What's wrong?"

I don't respond, but I do pick up my pace. When I reach the stairs, I lift Harlow over my shoulder and take the steps two at a time.

"Put me down," she cries at my back.

I smack her ass instead.

I take long strides down the hall to her room and remember that she keeps it locked. Reaching up to feel along her pockets, my fingers find the outline of a key. I get it and unlock the door, all while keeping my other arm around the back of her knees to keep her firmly in place.

After shutting the door, I set Harlow on her feet and take a step back to look her in the eyes.

Oh, she's pissed. Good. I want that fire right now. *Desperately.*

"Mala—"

"No talking," I growl.

I grab her by the shoulders and pull her into my chest, my hands moving to cup her face as I do. My lips press against hers, once, twice, three times.

"Here's how this is going to work," I begin, slowly

pushing her cut off her shoulders. "You're going to stand here, quietly, while I strip you."

I grab the hem of her shirt and drag it over her head.

"One."

I reach around and unsnap her bra.

"Piece."

Next, I grab her hatchet and tuck the handle into the back of my waistband.

Thank you Fiona for the idea.

"Of clothing."

I lean forward and trail the tip of my tongue around a nipple, then move to the next. All the while, I'm unbuttoning her pants and shoving them over her hips.

"At."

Licking down her stomach, I land on the top of her panties and drag them down her legs with my teeth.

"A time."

Harlow whimpers as I caress the inside of her thighs.

"Quiet, *bella*," I demand.

I lift each leg, one at a time, to help her step out of the clothes pooled around her ankles, and once she's free, I stand.

"Stand next to the end of the couch, facing the armrest."

Harlow hesitates.

"Now," I growl, the sound low, menacing.

She moves to stand exactly where I told her. I quickly strip out of my clothes, tossing them to the floor in a heap. But I keep the hatchet. I hold onto that thing like it's a life raft, and I just went overboard on the Titanic.

Taking myself in hand, I pump my cock a few times. "Fuck, I'm hard for you."

Harlow turns to look at me. We can't have that.

"Face forward."

Harlow's shoulders rise and fall, and I swear I can see her pulse at her throat. I take the pillows off of the bed and place them on the couch in front of her. Her eyes shift as she watches me, but other than that, she doesn't move.

When I move to stand at her back, I press my body into hers, lining us up, skin to skin.

"You're flushed, Harlow," I whisper in her ear. "And I bet your pussy is wet."

With my palm flat on her back, I bend her over the arm of the couch. Her upper body is supported by the pillows and her ass is in the air. Using my foot, I gently kick her legs apart.

Then, with my only goal being to tease her into oblivion using only her own weapon and my voice, I lift the hatchet and lay the flat of the blade against her upper back. Harlow gasps when the cold steel hits her skin, and goosebumps break out over her ass cheeks.

I tilt the weapon, careful not to let the sharp edge break skin, and slide it down. Lower, lower, slowly, agonizingly slow.

"Have you ever been given pleasure by something designed to give nothing but pain?"

Harlow shakes her head.

"You're about to."

I angle the hatchet so it's almost on end and glide it over one ass cheek and back up the other, in a horseshoe pattern. Harlow shivers with each pass of the end near the juncture of her thighs.

Deciding to give her pussy some attention, I drop to my knees and use my shoulders to spread Harlow's legs further apart so I can see what I'm doing.

Using the sharp edge of the blade, I tease her inner thigh, so lightly, I might as well be using a feather. I shift it upward, toward her pussy lips, and stop just shy of touching her. I repeat the action on her other side. Again and again, I taunt her.

"I can see your pussy glistening, Harlow." I inhale deeply. "And I can smell how bad you want me."

"Mmm," she moans.

It's on the tip of my tongue to reprimand her, but I don't. I just keep teasing, taunting, stimulating. Harlow's legs begin to shake, so I lower the hatchet to the floor.

Then I lean in close and blow on her clit.

"I wanna lick you, *bella.* I wanna drag my tongue over your clit and drink in your pleasure." Another breath.

Harlow's toes crack as she curls them. She's close. So fucking close. I wrap my hand around my cock, simply to keep it busy so I don't touch her. I don't know who I'm torturing more, her or me.

"And while I lick you, I'll fuck you with my fingers, curling them to reach that secret spot, that spot that no other man will ever touch again." Another breath, longer this time. "I'll make you come apart on my face, lap up everything you have to give me. And I'll do it happily, greedily."

I blow on her, a short puff of air, and Harlow's hips buck as she falls apart.

"That's it," I moan, still not touching her.

Once her body relaxes, I kiss one inner thigh, then the other. I nibble my way up and finally give in to what I need as I lick up her pleasure, exactly like I said I would.

Soft my ass.

CHAPTER 25
Harlow

HOLY HELL.

Malachi sure knows how to use that mouth of his. And who would've guessed my hatchet could be so stimulating?

"Stand up."

I shake my head. I don't think I can move.

"Harlow, I'm not done with you," he growls as he runs his hands over the globes of my ass and up my back. "Stand. Up."

I pull my arms in toward my chest to use them as leverage to stand. My legs wobble, but Malachi wraps an arm around my waist to steady me.

"This time, don't you dare be quiet," he whispers in my ear.

I shiver at the command. Malachi bends and lifts me up to carry me to the bed. When he lays me down across the mattress, he crawls over my body and staddles my hips, letting his thick cock rub against my core.

"Fuck," I hiss.

"You wanna fuck, Harlow?"

I nod.

"Say it," he snaps. "Tell me how you want me to fuck you."

I reach up and press my palms to his chest and then curl my fingers. I dig my nails into his flesh and drag them down toward his happy trail.

"I want you to fuck me, Malachi," I purr. "Hard, fast, long. I want you to fuck me to the point where I don't even know my name anymore. I want you to fuck me and make me yours."

Malachi grins as he grips my wrists and lifts them to the headboard. "Hold on, Harlow. Things are about to get rough."

In a movement quick as a torpedo, Malachi lines himself up and impales me so hard I scoot up the bed. He holds himself still for a moment and then slowly drags himself back out until only the tip remains.

"Hard, Malachi," I beg. "More."

Malachi thrusts forward, holds, lazily retreats. He does this several times, working me into a fever pitch of passion.

"Please," I whimper. "Faster."

He repeats his earlier action twice more before giving me what I need. Malachi pistons in and out of me, filling me impossibly full. He undulates his hips as he thrusts, creating friction against my clit as he moves.

I throw my head back and moan as I lift my hips to meet his demanding rhythm. Malachi sets an almost impossible pace, but I keep up. I flex my muscles to squeeze his dick and a growl barrels out of his mouth.

"Fuck me, that feels good," he groans. "Come for me, *bella*. One more time before I let myself go. Touch yourself if you have to." His words are stilted, but the point is the same.

I reach between our bodies and rub circles over my clit as he dips his head and latches onto a nipple. Our hips are in sync, my finger and his tongue are in sync. *We're* in sync.

"Coming," I pant. "I'm coming."

Malachi thrusts harder as I spasm around him. "Yeah you are," he grunts. "So good. I'm gonna…"

His words trail off when he throws his head back and shouts out his release. Even my spasms and his pulses are in sync. Several delirious minutes pass before Malachi collapses on top of me and then rolls to the side, pulling me in his arms as he does.

"Harlow?"

"Hmm?"

"I will gladly give up control to you outside of the bedroom, but in here, it's mine. You're mine. Got it?"

Thank God.

I need to be in charge of my club, in control at all times, especially with how important what we do is. But when it comes to sex, I'll gladly submit. Over and over and over again.

"Got it."

———

"Harlow."

"Go away," I mumble.

I'm having the most incredible dream, and I do not want to wake up.

"Harlow, c'mon."

I push at the hand on my shoulder, the one shaking me when all I want to do is focus on the hard body pressed against mine.

"Harlow!"

I jackknife into a sitting position, torn from my dream. Only it's not a dream because two strong legs are wrapped around mine and when I look to my left, Malachi is laying there, still naked, with a smile on his face.

When I look to my right, I see Peppermint, her hand still on my shoulder.

"C'mon. Get dressed and get downstairs. Playtime's over." She glances at Malachi. "You too, big boy."

She flashes Malachi a smirk before turning on her heel and striding out of the room. I make a mental note to bitch slap her later for peeking at my man's junk.

My man?

"Guess I forgot to lock the door," Malachi says half-heartedly.

"Yeah ya did," I mutter.

Five minutes later, we're both dressed and striding into the main room downstairs. Peppermint is sitting at one of the tables, along with Spooks and Mama. Peppermint waves me over.

When Malachi and I reach them, we swipe two chairs from the nearest table and slide them up so we can sit with the girls.

"What's up?" I ask.

"Mama and I went on a liquor run," Spooks begins. "And when we came back, Vinnie said this was dropped off for Malachi by a courier service. Didn't even know that was a real job."

She hands me an envelope. Malachi Ricci is typed on the front, but it's otherwise blank. I hand it to him.

"Any clue what it could be?" I ask him as he rips it open.

"Nope." He pulls out several pieces of paper, reads the top one and then gives it to me. "It's from Nico."

I read the typed note.

Mal,

Your father's will is enclosed. The one he had drawn up when you were born. It's been updated numerous times, but I can make all the updates disappear. Let me know.

Nico

"Call him," I tell Malachi.

Malachi does and Nico answers on the second ring.

"Ya got it?"

"Yeah, but why the cloak and dagger shit?" Malachi asks. "Why not just call and tell me? Or text? You know they can't trace your number, so don't give me that excuse."

I picture Nico shrugging with his next words. "This was more fun."

"You really need to stop watching old spy movies, Nico," Malachi mutters. "You're not a spy."

"If you say so."

"Both of you, stop," I bite out. "Nico, why would Malachi need the old will?"

"Because in the old one, all of my father's assets are left to me," Malachi answers instead of Nico. "After Mina was the first time he updated it. Took me out of it completely."

"But if those updates didn't happen…" Nico hints.

"I get it, Nico. And this helps us how?"

"All the money will funnel to me. My father updated it when Mortichi was born to leave him the house. But when Mortichi died, he updated it again to leave the house to Uncle Angelo."

"Great, so you're even more rich than you were yesterday. Still not seeing how this keeps you alive."

"It's a bargaining chip," Peppermint says.

"Exactly," Nico agrees.

Peppermint glares at Malachi's phone, which is sitting in the middle of the table, no doubt wishing the voice coming through the speaker was a person in front of her who she could throttle, then gets up to walk away. I make a mental note to talk to her when I get off the phone. I know this is hard for her.

"Looks like we're going back to the drawing board," I say, annoyed that the plan keeps changing. When I walked out of church earlier, I felt good, solid.

Now, not so much.

"Make the updates disappear," I instruct Nico. "I want it as if they never existed."

"Malachi, you good with this?" Nico asks.

Malachi looks to me as if searching for answers to questions that haven't even been asked. I only give him an encouraging nod.

"I'm good," Malachi says and disconnects the call.

"Let's go plan," I say as I stand. "Church, now!" I call out to the room, loud enough for the officers to hear over the music.

I grab Malachi's hand and usher him toward the meeting room. It's unconventional to have him there, but I don't feel right keeping him out of the loop anymore. I don't know what changed between this morning and now, but...

Everything changed. Absolutely everything.

Club business will always remain club business, but if it pertains to him, he'll know about it.

We won't stand a chance otherwise. Too many secrets are bad for a relationship.

Relationship?

Yeah, I thought what I thought.

Motherfucking relationship.

CHAPTER 26

Malachi

"ARE YOU SURE ABOUT THIS?"

Harlow's been pacing my office at Umbria's Universe for the last twenty minutes. I gave up watching because I was going to get whiplash. Instead, I started clearing out files from my computer.

"We've been over this, Harlow, time and time again. I'm sure."

She comes to a halt in front of my desk and puts her hands on her hips. It's weird seeing her without her hatchet, but she agreed to my request that she leave it in my car for this meeting. Granted, it was an argument, but she caved. I will thank her for that later.

"But this is your—"

"Stop," I snap, tired of the same conversation. "I'm sure."

Harlow huffs out a breath. "Okay."

"But no surprises this time, *bella.* We stick to the plan. Both of us."

"I will. I promise."

The door to my office swings open, and Gill walks in.

"They're here," he says.

"Weapons?" I ask.

"Confiscated them."

"Sure about that?" Harlow asks him.

Gill glares at her. "Seeing as I didn't have to wrestle a damn hatchet, yeah, I'm sure."

She shrugs. "Just checking."

"Harlow," I growl. "Not now."

She huffs out a breath, but nods.

"Let's get this over with," I say and walk around my desk to lace my fingers with Harlow's.

"Still want me there?" Gill asks as he follows us down the hall toward the conference room.

"Yes."

We reach the room, and I pause to take a deep breath. I'm confident that this will work. My uncle is too greedy for it not to. Harlow rises onto her tiptoes and presses a kiss to my ear.

"We got this," she whispers.

Damn straight we do.

I nod at Gill to open the door for us to enter. Not because I can't do it myself. It's calculated, a power move.

I step into the conference room, and sitting at the table is Uncle Angelo, Nicholi, and my father's attorney.

"Gentlemen," I say. "Thank you for coming."

"What the hell is this about, Malachi?" Uncle Angelo snarls. "It's bad enough we had to bury your father yesterday, but now you're demanding meetings with us."

"I didn't demand anything," I correct, my eyes bouncing between my uncle and cousin. "I simply requested that the reading of the will be completed here, rather than at the house. I'm sure you can understand why."

Neither of them says a word, because then they'd have to forgo whatever it is they think they're getting today. As far as anyone outside the family is concerned, my father's cancer is what killed him.

I pull a chair out for Harlow, and she sits. I take the seat next to her. Gill remains by the door, arms crossed over his chest, basically just looking mean.

I turn to the attorney. "Mr. Temple, please proceed."

Mr. Temple passes copies of the will to each of us present, Harlow included, and then clears his throat.

"As discussed and agreed upon by all parties, I'll go through the will in bullet point fashion."

"I appreciate it," I say, trying to be cordial.

"Just get on with it, Temple," Uncle Angelo grates out.

"Yes, well, the first order of business is the main residence. That will pass on to Angelo Ricci. The residence in Venice will pass on to Nicholi Ricci." Nicholi grins, but I ignore it. So far, so good. Temple goes on to list some collector's items I couldn't give two shits about, then he gets to the good stuff. "As for the financial assets, which have a sum total of twenty-two million dollars, those have already been transferred to accounts in the name of…"

Temple stares at the paper in front of him, mouth agape. Angelo and Nicholi are staring at Temple, not bothering to look at their own copies. And me? I'm leaning back in my chair, comfortable as can be, without a care in the world.

Thank you, Nico.

"That can't be right," Temple murmurs, shaking his head. "I know this isn't right."

"What's not right, Mr. Temple?" I ask, feigning concern.

"Temple, what's going on?" Angelo demands. He lifts his own copy, finally, and his face reddens to what should be an impossible degree.

Temple lifts his eyes to mine and then drops them again to look at the will he's holding.

"This isn't the will I drew up for Antonio six months ago when his cancer started progressing."

"How is that possible?" I ask.

"Could it have been a mix up by a secretary or something?" Harlow suggests, ever helpful.

"No, no. I printed my own copies before I left the office," Temple insists. "This is a terrible mistake." He reaches into his inside suit pocket and pulls out his cell phone. "I'm just going to call the office really quick and have someone pull up the files on my computer. We'll get this straightened out."

"Take your time." I say.

Twenty minutes later, after a lot of cussing and sweating on Temple's part, he disconnects the call.

He looks at Angelo. "There's no mistake. Every copy of the will, they all say the same thing."

"Impossible," Angelo huffs out.

"And what does the will say, Mr. Temple?" I ask. "I really would like to get this business out of the way."

Temple takes a deep breath and stares at the document. "All financial assets, totaling twenty-two million dollars have been transferred into accounts in the name of…" He swallows. "… Malachi Ricci."

I can't stop my grin. "Wow. I didn't realize Father regarded me in such high esteem."

"Oh, cut the bullshit, Malachi," Angelo snaps, shooting to his feet. "You did this somehow, I just know it."

I see Gill move to the end of the table out of the corner of my eye, closer to my uncle.

"And how would I do that? I've either been here or at the DHMC clubhouse all week. If you'd like to verify that, I can arrange for you to view the security footage of both places."

Nicholi glares at his father. "You said the money was coming to us. You said we'd be set with Uncle Antonio gone."

"Shut up, boy!" Angelo shouts, bringing his fists down on the table and then glaring at me. "You're a dead man, Malachi."

I tilt my head casually. "I thought I already was. From what I hear, you've already put a hit out on me." I glance at the attorney and force my face to register an 'oh shit' expression. "Oops. Probably shouldn't have said that in front of

Temple here." I shrug. "Guess it's a good thing he's on the payroll. Or is it? I'm not quite sure how you plan on paying him now that I have all the money."

Temple's eyes sharpen on my uncle. "What's he talking about?"

"I'll spell it out for you, Temple," I say shrewdly as I lean forward on the table. "My family hates me, wants me dead in fact. And since I now control the money, they have no means to pay the bills. I suppose they could sell the houses, liquidate the physical assets, but that takes time." I know Temple understands what I'm saying, but he's still glancing between me and my uncle as if that will change the facts. "In laymen's terms, they're fucking broke."

"Is this true?" Temple asks Angelo. "How is this possible? You assured me that you'd be able to maintain my services."

Uncle Angelo remains silent, but he glares at me with so much hate and rage that I feel it all the way to my bones.

And I love it.

I stand from my chair. "Now, I have a proposition for you, *Uncle*. One that could take away all your troubles."

"There's nothing you could—"

Uncle Angelo swings his arm and backhands Nicholi so hard my cousin's head whips to the side and blood flies from his lip.

"Ouch." I pretend wince. "Still don't know when to keep your mouth shut, do ya Nicholi? Pity."

My uncle straightens his suit jacket. "What makes you think you have anything I'm interested in?" he asks me.

I whistle. "I don't know. Most people would have their interest piqued by twenty-two million dollars." I glance at Harlow and wink before returning my stare to Angelo. "Guess you're not most people."

Uncle Angelo seems to consider this for a moment and then gives a curt nod. "I'm listening."

"I thought you might," I tell him. I glance at Temple.

"Might want to jot this all down. I'm sure your client will want something legally binding. Or as legal as you can make it, considering who you work for." Taking a deep breath, I savor the seconds that tick by with Angelo squirming. "I'm willing to give you everything."

Wide eyes stare back at me. "Everything?"

"Everything," I confirm. "I'll even throw in Umbria's Universe because I'm such a nice guy."

"Nice guy, my ass," Nicholi mutters.

"No one gives up that much without wanting something in return," Uncle Angelo states.

"Now that you mention it…"

"What do you want? What the fuck is all this going to cost me? Because we both know you're not doing this out of the goodness of your heart."

I sigh dramatically. "You're right, of course. Pretty sure any goodwill I had toward the family died a slow death ten years ago." Clapping my hands together, I grin. "So, all of this can be yours for the low, low price of…" I mimic a drumroll. "... Taking the target off my back."

"You can't be serious?"

"As a slit throat, Uncle."

"Malachi," Harlow interrupts as planned. "I think you're forgetting something."

"I wondered what the bitch was doing here," Uncle Angelo says snidely.

Gill strides to Angelo and wraps a meaty arm around his neck, cutting off his air supply. Nicholi shoots to his feet and throws a punch at Gill, but Gill dodges the blow and Nicholi's fist hits the side of his father's head.

"Her name is Harlow," I snarl, leaning on my outstretched arms. "Understood?"

Angelo nods.

"Good."

I nod at Gill to release the man, and when he does, Angelo gulps for air.

"And here things were going so well." I tsk. "But Harlow's right. I did forget one thing."

"What?"

"You leave the Devil's Handmaidens alone. No war, no retaliation for anything they've ever done, nothing."

"I want the treaty ripped up," Angelo counters.

"Not that you respected it anyway, but done."

Angelo slides his stare to Harlow. "Do you agree to that? We rip up the treaty, both of us free to go about our business as we wish?" Angelo smirks. "Without a target on my nephew's back and no war between the two organizations, of course."

"Sounds good to me," Harlow quips.

Angelo looks as if he's considering my proposition, but I know he's not. He'd be a fool not to accept. And he's greedy. The money is all he cares about, so I know what his answer will be before he even opens his mouth.

Still, it's music to my ears when I hear him speak.

"Done."

CHAPTER 27
Harlow

"NICE WORK, PREZ."

I smile across the table at Spooks.

"Thanks, but it was all Malachi."

As planned, Malachi and I returned to the clubhouse following the meeting with Angelo and Nicholi so I could provide an update to the club. I just finished filling them in, so now we can focus on phase two.

I look at our secretary. "Story, catch us up."

Story looks up from her laptop screen. "I finished up with Nico just before you got back. All the money was transferred to Angelo. Nico made sure to maintain his access to the accounts so we can easily funnel it back when it's time."

"Good. What about communication? Anything yet?"

"It's pretty insane, really. Nico found an email Angelo sent within minutes of leaving the casino calling off the hit on Malachi. But a few minutes later, he placed a call to a known gun for hire. Unless that was a booty call, Malachi's still a target."

"We knew that was a possibility," I remind her. "What about the trafficking? The treaty is officially null and void, so

I'm sure Angelo's chomping at the bit to get that back up and running now that the funeral is over."

"Nothing has changed on the schedule, but Nico and I are monitoring it carefully."

"Fox and several others are patrolling the stash house neighborhoods," Peppermint says. "They'll let us know if anything pops before we go in."

"Which brings us to the raids," I say. "According to Malachi, there are four stash houses scattered throughout the county. They aren't heavily guarded, only two men stationed at each."

"Stupid," Spooks spits out. "We can take them out easily."

"We can," I confirm. "But this is bigger than just taking out the guards. We need to be careful because these are residential neighborhoods, which means witnesses. We also have to get the victims out, and we all know from experience that that isn't always easy. They're already scared, tired, hungry, and who knows what else, and then here we come, another unknown entity. It takes a hot minute for them to recognize we mean them no harm."

"Not our first rodeo, Prez," Mama comments. "We've got this."

"I know we do." I take a deep breath. "I just…"

"This is different." I whip my head around to look at Giggles, and she shrugs. "It is. We're not just doing this for the victims. We're doing this for Malachi, too." She pauses, softens her features. "And Velvet."

I close my eyes at the mention of my mom. They all know my mom's story, why she died. I told them because they needed to know. Because it's not just my history, it's part of the club's as well.

So yeah, we're doing this because it's what we do. We're doing this to help Malachi get revenge. And we're doing it to get revenge for Velvet.

"For Velvet," Peppermint says.

"For Velvet," everyone repeats.

I reign in my thoughts and focus on the here and now.

"Does everyone have their assignments?" I ask.

"Yeah," Peppermint says. "Spooks, Giggles, Mama, and Tahiti will each have their own team. One team per location. You and I will handle Angelo, Nicholi, and anyone else who might be at that monstrosity they call a house."

"Malachi and Gill, along with Malachi's supporters, will take out anyone else tied to the trafficking. Not everyone in the organization plays a role in that particular endeavor, so some will be left alone."

"Any questions?" I ask. When there are none, I say, "Okay. We ride out tomorrow at midnight. Those going to the stash houses, you've got the vans. The rest of us, Harleys are not optional. Take the rest of the day and chill. Drink, fuck, sleep, I don't care. But tomorrow, you prepare. Make sure your weapons are ready, the vans are stocked with supplies, and your head is in the game. Because once we leave our property, there's no turning back. This is the largest mission we've ever run, and there's no room for error if we want to eliminate the Italians once and for all." I scan the eyes of each of my sisters, nodding at them as I do. "Dismissed."

Chairs scrape across the floor as each of them stand, and I watch them walk out of the room. Everyone but Peppermint.

"What's up, Pep?" I ask her.

"If he's there, he's mine." Her voice is quiet but filled with steel.

"You think you'd recognize him after all these years?"

"Har, you don't forget the face of the person who destroyed you."

"Okay, Pep. If he's there, he's yours." I hate this for her. "But if he's not? What then?"

She averts her eyes and stares at the wall for a moment. I know she's reliving every moment she was at the mercy of the Italians. It may have been a decade ago, but in her mind, it might as well have been yesterday.

When she returns her gaze to me, tears cling to her lashes, and she shrugs. "I'll have to deal with it."

"Not alone, Pep. You'll never have to deal with it alone. You know that, right?"

Finally, her lips tilt into a small smile. It's sad, but I'll take it. "I know the club has my back, Har. They always do."

"Not just the club. You've got me. I'll never let you go through anything alone."

"You love me, I know."

"I..." I nod. "Yeah."

Peppermint wipes under her eyes and takes a deep breath. When she exhales, she pastes a grin on her face, and it's as if this conversation never took place.

"Go get your man," she says. "I'm sure you've got things you want to do with him."

Peppermint winks before stepping around me and walking out of the room. I turn to watch her leave, a heaviness settling in my gut.

I drop my chin and stare at the floor. I'm worried about her. That's not anything new, though. I've worried about her since the moment my mom told me to take care of her. But this, the Italians? This isn't good. We've never had reason to go up against them until now. She's never had reason to potentially see her tormentor until now.

That's not true. You had plenty of reasons.

"You okay?"

I lift my head and see Malachi striding toward me. I force a smile and nod.

"Bullshit," he says. "Something's wrong."

Heaving a sigh, I debate on what to say to him. I don't want to lie, but how do I explain something that isn't up to me to explain?

"I'm worried about Pep," I settle on.

Malachi tilts his head. "Why?"

"Because she's my best friend, and tomorrow night is gonna be a wild one."

"Peppermint's solid. She can handle anything." He frowns. "Right?"

I chuckle. "Yeah, she's solid. And she'll have my back if that's what you're hinting at. I trust her with my life. So should you."

Malachi grabs my cut and tugs me to him. "Are you sure we have to split up tomorrow?"

He's asked me this so many times since we originally hatched the plan. And my answer remains the same.

"Yes."

He growls. "I don't like not being there to protect you. Why can't you and I go together, and Peppermint can go with Gill?"

"We agreed on this, Malachi," I remind him. "I can take care of myself. I need the strongest people taking the lead with each of the teams, which means you've got to take the lead with Gill. He's growing on me, but I still bested him so not sure I want him to be in charge of anything."

"Peppermint can take the lead then," he insists.

"Peppermint's with me," I snap, getting frustrated. I rise up on my tiptoes to kiss him in an effort to soften the moment. "I need you to do this for me, Malachi. Please? It's the only way I'll be satisfied that everything will get done the way it needs to get done."

"You play dirty, *bella*," he chastises playfully.

I grin. "I've got some time to play dirty for real," I tease.

Malachi leans back to lock eyes with me. His pupils are dilated, and his nostrils are flared.

"Upstairs. Now."

CHAPTER 28

Malachi

ONE HOUR BEFORE THE RAIDS...

"WHAT I WOULDN'T GIVE to be there for this."

I'm watching Harlow from across the room while I talk to Nico on the phone. She's dressed to kill... literally. Tight jeans, black boots, long-sleeved green tee and her cut encase her body perfectly. Her hatchet is strapped to her hip, as are several other knives. There's a gun strapped to her thigh as well.

Looking at her now, it's hard to believe I ever thought her look was 'biker bitch'. Oh, she's all biker for sure, but she's sexy as fuck and pushes all of my buttons.

"You'll be here soon," I tell my cousin as I adjust my cock.

"Just doesn't seem fair that I'm not the one who gets to end my father and brother," he complains.

"It's not fair, but it is what it is. Until we eliminate everyone, you're not safe here."

"But you going out tonight is safe?"

I sigh. I understand Nico's frustration. He's always been on the outside looking in, forced to act from the sidelines. But I didn't create the situation. I will end it though.

"I've been in this world a lot longer than you, Nico," I remind him.

"Just make sure Harlow knows to cut them up nice and slow," he demands darkly.

"I think she got that memo the first ten times you told her, but I'll remind her again."

"Thank you."

Harlow starts walking toward me, her eyes lighting up when she sees me staring.

"I think we're about to head out, Nico. I'll have the mic and earpiece in place in a few. Make sure you keep those directions coming."

Nico is essentially my base command tonight. He'll be guiding me and Gill as we traipse through the city taking out as many of the organization as we can.

"I will. Be careful, Malachi. I'm kinda looking forward to that hug."

"Me too, cousin. Me too."

I disconnect the call and open my arms so Harlow can step into them when she reaches me. She doesn't disappoint.

"You ready?" I ask her, resting my chin on her head.

"Always. You?"

"Always."

"When it's over, we'll meet back here."

"I know."

"And don't do anything stupid. Stick to the known targets. We can go out for stragglers later if we have to."

"Okay."

"If you run into trouble, mak—"

"Harlow, stop." I step back from her so I can look into her eyes. "We've been over this a dozen times. I know how to fight. I know how to take a life. I know what I'm doing."

"Yeah, but y—"

"No buts," I snap. "I'm trained, same as you. I'll be fine."

"Just come back to me, okay?"

"I will."

"Okay."

"Now, I need you to do the same. Be careful. No unnecessary risks. Get in, slice and dice, get out. Got it?"

"Slice and dice?" she asks, her lips twitching.

"What? It's what you do."

"I'll be careful. Angelo and Nicholi won't know what hit 'em."

I hear my name being called and look toward the door to see Gill waving to get my attention.

"I gotta go, *bella.*"

Harlow's face hardens, but it's not out of anger or any emotion directed at me. No, my biker chick is stepping into battle mode.

I fuse my lips to hers and dart my tongue into the recesses of her mouth. I show her exactly what she means to me in that kiss. When I pull away, I grin at the flush on her cheeks.

"See ya soon, Harlow."

CHAPTER 29

Harlow

FIVE MORE MILES.

I glance to my left and see Peppermint focused on the road in front of us. We all dispersed from the clubhouse around eleven thirty, going in our assigned directions. I'd be lying if I said it was easy to watch Malachi go the opposite way from me, but it had to be that way. I'll see him soon.

Three miles.

As the wind whips my face, I run through the blueprints of the house in my mind. I've been inside before, but Peppermint hasn't. She and I spent time going over the layout earlier today, so I'm not worried about that, but it never hurts to mentally review.

One mile.

Malachi asked me why Peppermint and I were riding our Harleys for the mission, and suggested we take a car instead. His argument was that he thought a quieter approach would be better. The *art of surprise* he called it.

I laughed in his face and told him I wanted the fuckers to hear us coming. I wanted them to shake with fear.

When the driveway comes into view, I slow the bike to make the turn. I don't know if Angelo and Nicholi, or any of the Italians for that matter, are afraid of us, but they should be.

I park my Harley in front of the walkway that leads to the steps and Peppermint pulls up beside me.

"You ready?" I ask my VP.

She pulls her knives from her belt, holds them out in front of her, and grins. "You have no idea."

"Then let's do this."

I race up the walkway, up the steps, and grip the doorknob, smiling when it turns with ease. Nico really is good. He said he'd have the security system shut down before our arrival and he delivered.

Thank you, Nico.

Peppermint and I stride into the house like we own the place. I expected to be greeted by guards or hell, even the butler, but the foyer is empty. I signal to my right before moving to enter the parlor where I was forced to wait the last time I was here.

"Where are they?" Peppermint asks when room after room is empty.

"They're here somewhere, we just have to keep going."

Ten minutes later, we've cleared the entire house and are standing back at the foyer. We're missing something, I know we are.

"Harlow, I really want to kill someone," Peppermint seethes. "Tell me this isn't a fool's errand."

"It's not," I snap a moment before it hits me. "Safe room."

"There was nothing on the blueprints," Peppermint reminds me.

"Would you put a safe room in blueprints?" I shake my head. "I wouldn't."

I pull out my cell and call Nico.

"Kinda busy," he says upon answering.

"I know and I won't keep you," I say quickly. "But the house is empty. We're thinking there's a safe room. If you disabled the security system, would that include a safe room? Or would they still be able to lock themselves inside."

"It's a safe room, Harlow. They should be able to lock themselves inside no matter what."

"And under what circumstances would the lock to the safe room not work?"

The tapping of a keyboard comes through the line for a moment before he speaks. "A power outage, maybe. But the window to get in would be minimal. You'd only have a minute or two between when the power is cut and any backup power source kicks on. And trust me, there's a backup source."

"Got it. Can you cut the power?"

"Of course," he huffs out, seemingly miffed at the question.

"I'll text you when I'm ready. Thanks, Nico."

I disconnect the call and look at Peppermint. "Now we just have to figure out if there is a safe room."

"Right, like that'll be easy. This place is massive."

"Then we better get to searching."

"If it were me, I'd keep it close to the room I use the most. Quickest access. So, what room would that be?"

I think about Malachi's father. He was sick and spent a lot of time confined to a bed, according to Malachi, but the safe room would have been built before his diagnosis so…

"The office."

I take off down the hallway, one after the other, until I come to the same stupid double doors I stared at before. Fuck, they really are ugly.

I hold a finger up to my lips before Peppermint and I silently slip inside the room. I take one half of the room while she takes the other. We inspect everything, from the wall sconces to each individual book on the shelves.

Getting frustrated, I move from the filing cabinet I just cleared to the approximately five-foot expanse of wall. And then I see it, the tiny imperfection in the way the wallpaper is lined up. Everything in this house is immaculate, perfect down to the smallest detail. So why isn't this?

"Pep," I whisper. "Got it."

She moves to my side while I text Nico.

Now!

I count the seconds that pass while we wait for darkness.

One.

Two.

Three.

C'mon, Nico.

Four.

Five.

Six.

What's taking so long?

Seven.

Eight.

The lights go out and a click echoes in the dark. I assume it's the door popping open because I can't see shit. Gunshots ring out, and I dive to the side to avoid bullets, hoping Peppermint does the same. The sound of each shot is deafening and reminds me why I prefer my hatchet. Sure, screams are loud, but the act of killing is not.

"You're making a big mistake," Angelo shouts from his hideout when the lights blink on.

I lift my head and see Peppermint still flat against the floor. Blood is trickling from a gash on her temple and she's motionless.

"I don't think so," I counter as I scramble to my friend.

I keep my hatchet gripped in my hand, ready to defend myself. Pressing a finger to Peppermint's throat, I feel for a pulse.

Thank fuck!

"Come out here, both of you, and face us like men," I demand. "Or are you too afraid of two chicks with blades?"

Surprisingly, Angelo steps around the door, gun aimed at my head. "Didn't your mom ever teach you not to bring a knife to a gunfight?" he snarls.

Pepper groans beside me as she comes around, so I shift all of my attention to Malachi's uncle.

"My mother taught me plenty. About guns and knives." I tilt my head. "For example, that gun you're holding has a standard seventeen bullets, all of which you've shot. 'Always count the number of shots, Harlow', she used to say. Now, I assume you have more ammo back there in your cave, and you could go for it. But do you really think you'll get far before I take you out with this?" I lift my hatchet.

Angelo stares at me as if mentally calculating his odds. Based on the fact that he doesn't move, I'd say he realizes they aren't great.

"Where's Nicholi?" I ask. "Get him out here."

Angelo looks at me as if he's bored. "I'd love to, but as soon as the door opened, he took off." He glances at Peppermint. "Got in one good hit though."

Dammit!

Out of the corner of my eye, I see Peppermint get to her feet. She sways slightly, but quickly steadies herself. Then she fixes her stare on Angelo and glares.

"Your son's a pussy," she spits out. "He knew the only way he could get past us was in the dark."

"My son did what he had to do," Angelo sneers. "That's more than I can say for my nephew. Where is he by the way?"

"Busy," I reply tightly.

Angelo drops his gun to the floor and raises his arms above his head. Then his mouth spreads into a grin. "Go ahead, kill me."

Something isn't right. He's giving up. Why the fuck is he giving up?

"What's so funny?" Peppermint barks.

"Nothing," Angelo says casually. "I'm just prepared to die. And I'll do it happily knowing my son is out there some- where, hiding, waiting, calculating his revenge." His grin widens. "And then there's the little matter of knowing I'll get to see my nephew again when I cross to the other side."

"What are you talking about?"

He's referring to Mortichi. Not Malachi. Malachi is fine. He's definitely referring to Mortichi.

My feet won't move. Despite my brain screaming at my body to act, to end this fuck's life, I can't goddamn move.

Seeing me freeze, Peppermint lunges forward and thrusts her knife into Angelo's stomach. When he laughs, she twists the handle.

"What did you do?" she snarls in his face.

Angelo coughs and blood spurts from his mouth. "I hand…" Cough. "Handled business."

Malachi!

Vibrations in my pocket pull me from my trance. I grab my phone and see a text from Nico.

Hit man struck. Malachi hurt. Hospital.

Seeing the information, right there in black and white, shocks me into action.

"Peppermint, move," I order, my tone calm, deadly so.

When she steps to the side, she yanks her blade out and wipes it on her jeans. I shift forward to take her place and squat down so I'm at eye level with Angelo.

"See you in Hell."

Then, with hands that have never been so steady, I grip my hatchet and slice it across his throat. Blood pours from the wound as he crumbles into a heap on his side. I raise my weapon and swing it down to cut through every inch of flesh and bone, over and over and over again. I hack him up until he's unrecognizable. And with every swing, I avenge anyone who has suffered at this man's hands, at the hands of those related to him.

"Harlow!"

I stop mid-swing and lift my eyes to see Peppermint holding her cell phone.

"What?"

"We need to go. Malachi needs you."

Malachi. Hit man. He's hurt. He needs me.

I return my attention to the corpse of pure evil and spit on it.

"Slice and dice, motherfucker."

CHAPTER 30

Malachi

"HOW DID THIS HAPPEN?"

I hiss when the nurse pulls out another piece of shrapnel, but my eyes track Gill, who's pacing the small cubicle in the emergency room. Everything went according to plan after we left the clubhouse earlier. Gill and I hit the first house, then the second, and the third. Between the two of us, and the six other men Nico was coordinating, we took out a total of sixteen supporters of the sex trafficking. Our execution was flawless.

Unfortunately, there's no way we could have prepared for what happened next. Gill and I strode out of the last man's house, exhausted and ready to head back. All I could think about was seeing Harlow, wrapping myself around her and sleeping for days.

"Would you sit down?" I bark at Gill. "You're giving me a headache."

He flops into the only chair cramped into the small space.

"We can discuss what went wrong later," I tell him, tilting my head toward the nurse.

Understanding my silent communication, he nods.

For the next ten minutes, we both sit silently while the nurse removes the rest of the shrapnel.

"I've got to get a few more supplies, but I'll be back to treat the burns."

She slips around the curtain at the same time a commotion breaks out on the other side of the barrier.

"Where is he!"

"Harlow's here," Gill says unnecessarily.

"Thanks," I reply dryly.

"Get your hands off me. I'm fine! I wanna see him."

"I'm in here," I call out, needing to see her.

The curtain is whipped to the side and in walks Harlow, covered in blood and madder than hell.

"Fucking pricks," she mutters. "I don't give a shit if I'm family or not." She raises her voice. "If I wanna see someone, I'm gonna see them!" she shouts.

I spare a glance at Gill, who's still sitting, but his brows are raised to his hairline.

"I don't think they were trying to stop you because you're not family, Harlow," I say. "Have you looked in a mirror at all?"

"What?"

"Your covered in blood, carrying a hatchet covered in blood, and you're raising hell," Gill says and then wisely presses his lips together when she shoots him a glare.

"Your point?" she snaps.

"He's trying, *and failing*, to tell you that the staff here at this fine establishment are simply trying to do their jobs and make sure you're not hurt."

All anger fades and Harlow's shoulders drop. "Oh."

"You're not hurt, right?" I ask.

"No, of course not." She takes the few steps to the side of the gurney I'm sitting on. "How are you?"

"I'll be fine. Got hit with some shrapnel, but the nurse removed it all. They're going to treat my burns. Should be good to go after that."

"What the fuck happened?"

"Later, *bella.*"

Harlow's eyes narrow, but she doesn't push. She does, however, whirl on Gill.

"And where the hell were you?"

"Harlow, don't," I warn, my patience wearing thin. I know she's worried, but Gill works for me, not her.

"Where were you?" she demands again.

"Harlow," I bark. "Look at me." She turns around. "It's not your job to chastise my men, or man in this case. This is not Gill's fault."

Harlow takes a deep breath, rocks on her heels, and then nods. "Fine."

"Now, have you heard from the others?" I ask, needing to know the rest of the raids weren't a cluster-fuck like mine.

"Yeah. They've all checked in. Everyone's getting settled at Devil's Double Down."

"Angelo and Nicholi?"

Before she can answer, the nurse returns to tend to my burns. Another two hours passes before I'm released with care instructions. The three of us walk into the parking lot, straight toward Peppermint, who's standing next to both her and Harlow's Harleys.

"I want answers," Harlow says now that we're out of earshot of anyone else.

I take a deep breath, wincing at the pain it causes. "Car bomb."

"What?!"

"Everything was fine until we left the last house. As I was stepping off the curb, my car exploded. Gill was still on the porch, so he was far enough away. I wasn't that lucky." I wave my hand like it doesn't matter. "Anyway, as far as Nico can tell, at least in the few minutes we had to wait for an ambulance, it was the hired gun my uncle contracted with.

He must have trailed us all night and put the bomb in place while we were inside that last house. On the plus side, he's a shit hired gun. Bomb went off early and he was killed."

"Good."

"Angelo and Nicholi?" I ask.

Harlow and Peppermint exchange a look.

"Angelo's dead," Harlow says.

"Nicholi?"

Peppermint shakes her head. "He got away."

"How?"

"We had to have Nico cut the power," Harlow says, her tone cold. "He slipped out in the dark."

"Not before leaving a calling card though," Peppermint says, pointing to the gash on her head.

"You should probably have that looked at," I tell her.

"I'm fine."

I hitch a thumb over my shoulder. "We're at the hospital. Might as well get it—"

"I said I'm fine," Peppermint snaps.

"We've gotta get over to the casino and help out," Harlow says, steering the conversation to safer waters. "You both should tag along. See what you've been fighting against all these years."

I glance around the parking lot. "My car kinda blew up tonight, *bella*. How do you suppose we get there?"

Harlow darts her gaze between me and Gill, and then glances at Peppermint, arching a brow. Peppermint glares at Gill, but shrugs.

"Ride with us."

"You can't be serious."

"Why not?" Harlow crosses her arms over her chest. "What are you afraid of?"

"Nothing," I insist.

"I'm not getting on the back of no chick's bike," Gill argues.

Harlow huffs out a breath. "It's still dark out guys. No one will see you."

Gill and I exchange a look and I sigh.

"Fine. But only because I want my arms wrapped around you and this will make it happen faster," I tell her.

"I didn't agree to—"

"C'mon, Gill," Peppermint chortles. "I promise to keep you safe."

Gill groans, but stomps to stand next to the Harley as Peppermint staddles the bike. He turns to look at me before getting on behind her.

"You owe me for this, boss."

"How's a raise sound?"

"How much we talking?" he counters.

I shrug. "Don't know. Gotta run the numbers. But I'll make it worth your while."

"Fine," he mutters as he gets on behind Peppermint.

"You're turn," Harlow says when she's on her bike.

I stare at her for a moment, letting myself take in her perfection. Harlow's covered in blood, grinning from ear to ear, armed with a fucking hatchet, and wearing her cut with the president patch. And she's never been more beautiful.

I climb on behind her, and that's how I experience my first ride on a motorcycle. Riding bitch, with my arms full of my woman.

Epilogue

HARLOW

Six months later…

"WE HAVE another winner here at the Devil's Double Down…"

The rest of the announcement is drowned out by the banging of my office door against the wall. I turn from the large window and see Peppermint stride in with a pissed off expression.

Not again. How much more can she take?

"If Nico ever decides to show his face in this city again, I swear to fuck I'm gonna kill him with my bare hands."

I arch a brow at my best friend. "Another dead end, I take it."

Nico has yet to return from his forced exile. But to his credit, he's still helping from afar. He's been trying to find Nicholi, but every single lead he gives us leaves us empty handed. Malachi has his men on it too, but they're not getting anywhere either.

"If Malachi didn't speak so highly of Nico, I'd think he was setting us up," Peppermint grumbles.

"The thought has crossed my mind," I admit. "But Malachi assures me that Nico's solid. And after all the help he's given us, I think Nico's proven that."

Peppermint rolls her eyes. "Yeah, I know."

"You really don't like him, do you?"

"He's a Ricci," she says as if that explains everything. "What's there to like?"

"Malachi's a Ricci and you like *him*."

"Of course I do. But Malachi's different. He loves you, so he's safe from my hatred."

My heart squeezes at that word: love. Malachi has said it to me so many times, you'd think I'd be immune to the paralyzing hold it has on me, but no.

"I know he does," I say tightly.

Peppermint heaves a sigh and rises from her chair to walk closer to me. "Still haven't said it?"

I shake my head.

"Har, the man gave up his legacy for you. Shit, you both sold your condos and bought a house together last month. He's not going anywhere."

She's right, I know she is. Malachi did give up his legacy. The Ricci Crime Family is no longer. After all of the sex trafficking supporters were wiped out—well, other than Nicholi, of course—Malachi and Nico decided to go legit. The only remaining business from before we met is Umbria's Universe.

Malachi's hands are clean. He even used the money from his father to start his own security firm. They deal mostly in search and rescue overseas but help out DHMC when we need it. And Malachi always has a team, led by Nico, searching for Nicholi.

Life has been great. So why do I still get tongue-tied when it comes to telling him I love him? Because I do love him. It didn't take long to figure that out. The second I read that text from Nico about Malachi being hurt by a hit man, I froze.

I never freeze. Ever. But the thought of losing him, before we even really had a chance to start was terrifying. So yeah, I love him.

"Harlow, talk to me," Peppermint pushes when don't respond.

"I don't know what to say. This isn't a new problem, Pep. If I could fix it, I would."

She shakes her head. "Okay. I'll drop it for now."

Peppermint walks to the door but stops before walking out of my office. She looks over her shoulder and says, "Love ya, Har."

"Love you too."

When she grins, I narrow my eyes at her. "What?"

"Do you know what you just said?"

I think back. I said…

"Oh my God," I whisper, stunned.

"Yeah. I hate to break it to you, but you've been saying it to me for weeks. I didn't want to make a big deal out of it, so I didn't say anything, but I did call Malachi. Asked him if you said it to him yet. When he told me no, he sounded…" My best friend shrugs. "… broken. I knew I couldn't keep my mouth shut anymore."

"Weeks? Seriously?"

"Yep." She winks. "I'll give you a five-minute head start, but then I'm calling Malachi to tell him he's needed at home."

"Why?"

"Because you need to make this right. You need to tell that man you love him."

I don't even hesitate. I race past her out of my office and down the hall. Her laughter fuels me, and I run faster.

If I can tell Peppermint that I love her, surely I can tell Malachi.

Right?

It takes me ten minutes to get to our house just outside of the city. Fortunately, traffic wasn't bad. I rush inside and up the stairs, one destination in mind: our bedroom.

We decorated this room similar to my room at the clubhouse. Our bed is along one wall, while a loveseat is on another. Both get used… a lot.

I strip out of my clothes, stumbling when my jeans catch around my ankles. I kick my legs free and scramble to my feet. I move the pillows from the bed to the couch. And for the final touch, I'm holding our hatchet. We ended up having another one custom made specifically for play. The blade isn't killing sharp, so it's safer for the times we get out of control.

Peppermint was true to her word because I hear the garage go up two minutes later. Doors slam and bang throughout the house.

"Harlow!" Malachi yells. "Where are you? Harlow?"

I remain silent.

His footsteps on the stairs as he races toward me have my pussy clenching. Fuck this man does things to me. Our bedroom door flies open as Malachi barrels through.

And then he freezes.

"You're naked."

I nod.

Malachi blows out a breath. "Jesus, I thought you were hurt," he says. "Peppermint called and said I had to get home right away. All I could picture was Nicholi, here and—"

"I love you," I blurt.

Malachi tenses. "What?"

I take a deep breath. I'm gonna fuck this up, I just know it. But I have to do it.

"I've known since the moment I thought I was gonna lose you," I tell him. "I've never said it, and I should have. I should've told you as soon as I realized it. But I was scared." I swallow past the lump forming in my throat. Malachi stalks toward me as I talk. "I'm still scared. But not for the same reasons. I know you're not going anywhere. I know what we have is real. I know you love me. I'm still scared that I'll lose you to the evil in the world, but I can't control that. I can control whether or not you truly know how I feel. So starting now, I'll tell you every day."

Malachi cups my cheeks and presses a soft kiss to my lips. When he straightens, he smiles. "I've known you love me, *bella.* I feel it surrounding me all the time. I told you once that love isn't always about the words, but the actions. You show me every single day how you love me." He kisses my left cheek. "In the way you hug me." He kisses my right cheek. "In the way you watch me when you think I'm not looking." Tip of my nose. "In the way your arm wraps around my waist when you're sleeping." My chin. "In the way your eyes search for me in a room." My forehead. "In the way you try to protect me, even when I don't need it."

I nod, unable to speak.

"I always *feel* your love. But I can't tell you how happy it makes me to hear you say it."

"I do, Malachi. I love you so much it hurts."

"I love you, too."

I throw my arms around Malachi's waist and hold him tight. And his thick cock presses into my stomach, causing a shiver to race down my spine.

"Harlow?"

"Yeah?"

Malachi steps out of my hold and takes the hatchet from my hand.

"Stand next to the end of the couch, facing the armrest."

Next in the Devil's Handmaidens MC Series

Peppermint's Twist: Book 2
Coming February 2023

Peppermint...

My life has never been one of ease. Taken at fifteen, I was subjected to horrors better left in the dark, and then shunned by the people who were supposed to love me. Even with all that, I was one of the lucky ones. Because I was rescued by members of the very motorcycle club I am now proud to call my family.

But that doesn't mean I don't have scars. Deep, depressing, never-ending emotional pain forever reminds me of what I went through. That and the image of my tormentor, which is tattooed on my brain. It's been years since I've seen that face, but it's back. Only, it's different. The soul occupying the body isn't black as pitch. The man owning the body is a wise-ass, commanding, possessive, and a healthy dose of sweet and sin.

Can I trust the man with my tormentor's face? Or will he destroy me in ways I never dreamed?

Nico...

I'm the black sheep of a family who built their empire by treating humans like they're a commodity to be bought and sold. Banished at thirteen to spend my teenage years at a boarding school with no tether to the people I grew up with, all because I didn't conform to who they wanted me to be. But I was okay with that because at least I had a chance to be normal. And karma's a bitch.

My cousin and I planned for years to end the suffering our family caused and destroy those who caused it. We almost did it, too, but one member remains, still wreaking havoc on the city I call home again. Add in the fact that I've met the woman of my dreams, who happens to hate and fear me on sight, and life is a real barrel of laughs. No matter. I'll win her over and make her mine.

I just have to convince her that I'm not who she thinks I am and keep her alive long enough to do it.

About the Author

Andi Rhodes is an author whose passion is creating romance from chaos in all her books! She writes MC (motorcycle club) romance with a generous helping of suspense and doesn't shy away from the more difficult topics. Her books can be triggering for some so consider yourself warned. Andi also ensures each book ends with the couple getting their HEA! Most importantly, Andi is living her real life HEA with her husband and their boxers.

For access to release info, updates, and exclusive content, be sure to sign up for Andi's newsletter at andirhodes.com.

Also by Andi Rhodes

Broken Rebel Brotherhood

Broken Souls

Broken Innocence

Broken Boundaries

Broken Rebel Brotherhood: Complete Series Box set

Broken Rebel Brotherhood: Next Generation

Broken Hearts

Broken Wings

Broken Mind

Bastards and Badges

Stark Revenge

Slade's Fall

Jett's Guard

Soulless Kings MC

Fender

Joker

Piston

Greaser

Riker

Trainwreck

Squirrel

Gibson

Satan's Legacy MC

Snow's Angel

Toga's Demons

Magic's Torment